joanna

- a novel -

By Glen Dueck

FriesenPress

Suite 300 - 990 Fort St
Victoria, BC, Canada, V8V 3K2
www.friesenpress.com

Copyright © 2014 by Glen Dueck
First Edition — 2014

All rights reserved.

No part of this publication may be reproduced in any form, or by any means, electronic or mechanical, including photocopying, recording, or any information browsing, storage, or retrieval system, without permission in writing from the publisher.

Scripture taken from the New King James Version®.
Copyright © 1982 by Thomas Nelson. Used by permission.

ISBN
978-1-4602-5553-7 (Hardcover)
978-1-4602-5554-4 (Paperback)
978-1-4602-5555-1 (eBook)

1. *Fiction, Religious*

Distributed to the trade by The Ingram Book Company

Dedicated to my wife, Pauline
Whose support and constant love
is the wind beneath my wings

Acknowledgements:

Many thanks to Jana Joujan, free-lance author, Medicine Hat, AB for her very helpful work in content editing.

Also to Janell of Janell Allyn Photography, Medicine Hat, AB for her fine contribution to the cover.

Finally, to Kenya Gader, Medicine Hat, AB for being the perfect model (cover).

joanna

By Glen Dueck

Luke 8:1 Now it came to pass, afterward, that He went through every city and village, preaching and bringing the glad tidings of the kingdom of God. And the twelve were with Him, 2 and certain women who had been healed of evil spirits and infirmities—Mary called Magdalene, out of whom had come seven demons, 3 and Joanna the wife of Chuza, Herod's steward, and Susanna, and many others who provided for Him from their substance.

Chapter One

The Party

Joanna cast a lustful eye at the two soldiers dressed in Roman crimson. On any other day, they would have been standing motionless, as sentries to the entry to Herod's private quarters, but not today. Their responsibilities as soldiers now far from their minds, the two men swayed with the music of flutes and lyres, each with a woman by their side. Joanna took a second glance at one man with large, bulging biceps protruding from red sleeves decorated with several pennants and blue piping. She poked Mary in the side with her finger. "How do you like that one, Mary?"

Mary looked across the floor of dancers following Joanna's focus. "You mean the slim dancer?"

"No. Next to him... The one with the military cords — the blue trim."

"Oooh... Yes! Isn't he a wonderful sight! Almost too good-looking for a Roman!"

The light from several basin oil lamps flickered across the faces of men and women as they squealed with delight, augmented by the erotic music and the effects of too much wine. The flickering light intensified the mystic panorama of the night.

"Nobody throws a party like Herod, don't you think?" Joanna mused, and added, "I can't wait to get my arms around that soldier."

"Just make sure Chuza doesn't catch you!" Mary replied with a curled smirk on her face, "Husbands don't go much for flirting."

"Yes, but it's only true for their wives. Of course, husbands are the more chaste!" she mocked, quick to disregard any culpability in the matter.

"Isn't that so true!" Mary agreed.

"Seriously, Mary. I can't seem to find contentment in much these days. I hate Herod, sometimes Chuza, and most of the time, myself!"

"Lighten up a bit!" Mary tugged on Joanna's cloak, "Enjoy the moment. Eat, drink, and be merry!"

"If only I could," Joanna said truthfully.

"I need your key for the guest house. I'd like to stay the night. And don't forget you're coming to Magdala next week."

Joanna handed her the key. "Yes, in seven days we go to your town. I'll be glad to get away from here for awhile."

The sound of many shoes clattering on the marble floor of the palace echoed throughout the high ceiling. Joanna shook her head to clear her ears from the deafening roar and stretched her head back to gaze up at the images of

Jupiter and Zeus profiled against the gritty face of massive stone walls. Now letting her head drop, she took note of how the crowd had grown considerably over the last hour. She thought, I've been here longer than I realize, and smiled with satisfaction at the smell of wine mixed with royal dainties. The night was perfect for a party!

Joanna felt Mary's quick touch on her arm as she got up.

"It's time to make my move — Watch me!" giggled Mary.

Mary swung her slender yet well formed figure up off the bench and moved between the swarms of people on the floor. She had barely made five steps when a scuffle broke out in the corner. A crowd gathered around two common soldiers as they fought. Joanna's eyes followed as the two combatants endeavored to punch each other in the face while the crowd cheered them on. The taller fighter was stronger than the other, but what the smaller lacked in size, he made up for with gritty determination. The tall one grabbed the other by the back of his hair, while the shorter man jerked side to side. Soon they scuttled in a circle, the tall man still trying to get a fist in. Even though the taller man had a vice grip on him, he could not connect with any punches. There was a thud as the short man used his foot to make a crushing blow to the ribs of the other. The crowd gasped. The taller lost his grip for a moment, and when he grabbed the front of the short man, his nose received a calculated jab of the short man's fist. Several more punches ensued by both men. The crowd scrambled to get out of the way of flailing feet and arms. When they released their grip, both of them moved off to the side, glaring at each other.

"Just a fight," Joanna said out loud, "Good thing it wasn't a sword fight!" and several nearby nodded their agreement. The fight ended, and Joanna sighed. The event was a simple hand-to-hand wrestling match, urged on by hundreds of chanting madmen, but harmless enough. A broken wrist or nose would likely be the extent of their injuries.

Meanwhile, Joanna searched across the crowd for Mary. Where had she disappeared to? Joanna then caught sight of her, arm in arm with the soldier she had targeted, walking out the far gate and towards the streets of Tiberias.

Well! That didn't take long, she thought to herself.

She turned and spotted her husband, Chuza, coming across the floor, at the opening to Herod's quarters. He stopped, viewed the crowd, and gave a nod of approval to the chief food supplier. Now he walked over toward Joanna.

"Would you like to dance?" Joanna chirped, knowing Chuza was on duty, and the answer would be 'no'.

"That will definitely have to wait," He replied in his usual professional voice, as he marched up beside her. Even though Joanna knew he was on duty, her heart sank.

"Come on, Chuza! Have some fun—just once!"

Chuza gazed over the crowd methodically, undaunted by Joanna's request.

"We never do anything fun, Chuza! If not tonight, then when? You only think 'work, work, work!'" she needled. It wasn't because she despised Chuza, but his work as Herod's steward kept him busy, and too pre-occupied to spend much time with her. Chuza's silence echoed the emptiness in her heart.

Joanna spoke sarcastically, "Well, what do you propose I should do tonight? Sit here and watch the party unfold? Go take a nap? Count the number of guests for your records? Or should I tag along with you, on your exciting evening?"

With the last remark, Chuza frowned at her, and promptly turned his back. He started talking to one of the soldiers instead.

Joanna would never admit to him, but in recent days, her eyes had been more and more taken by others than him.

Partly Mary's fault, she decided. She's always out for the men. Mary may be a little devil at times, but she's the best friend I'll ever have, and I'll never give her friendship up!

Joanna took a last look at Mary as she disappeared into the night. She leaned her elbow on the stone fence in front of her, and gazed aimlessly at the crowd below.

She recalled how they had met at the most unlikely of places. During a summer rain storm a year ago, she had taken cover under the awning of one of the city's local vegetable shops. Mary, who lived in Magdala, happened to be in Tiberias at the same time, and had hoped to have a physician attend to her broken leg. At the first crack of thunder, she had hobbled over to the same vegetable shop where Joanna was.

Joanna had recognized Mary's plight, and couldn't help but feel sorry for her. While they had waited for the rain to stop, Joanna began the conversation.

"What happened?" she had asked, looking down at the bruises on her broken leg.

"I tripped over a rock while running," Mary had replied, smiling embarrassingly, "I love to run!"

Joanna had looked over the sleek and slender Mary, and noted she was nearly of athletic form. "You don't live in Tiberias, do you?" Joanna had asked, returning her smile. "Where are you from?"

"Oh, I live over in Magdala. You know, just down the road..."

"Of course. Yes, Magdala is a beautiful town. You must love the sound of the sea." Joanna had always thought Magdala to be a restful little town, and wished once-or-twice that she could live there. Even more, she had liked Mary's friendliness, and her easy-going personality.

Mary had continued, "Magdala is only a short way from here you know. Today it took me a good two hours to walk with help of my neighbor, but usually—well—maybe twenty or thirty minutes. I run, you know! I mean, usually I run." Mary had peered at her leg rather exasperated, with an odd mix of smile and grimace.

Soon the two of them had been talking about everything from home décor to what it was like to live next to the palace. Even though Mary was of lower class, Joanna had still befriended her. When one of the palace attendants with a donkey and cart passed by, she offered to take Mary to the palace for lunch.

The day they met had been the beginning of a long friendship. At every opportunity thereafter, Joanna had found a reason to walk the twenty-four furlongs from Tiberias, northward to Mary's home in Magdala. She loved the country walk, and the one hour trip didn't seem long at all.

Magdala is the perfect place to relax—by the Sea of Galilee, and no where near Herod, she had thought to herself.

Now her memories were interrupted as Chuza turned to face her. "Have you seen Crabolus?" Chuza inquired.

"Where the eagles fly, there you'll find a squawking duck! I expect if you find any of the dignitaries, you will find Crabolus squawking nearby."

"Incredibly witty, Joanna. But true," Chuza remarked. "Yes, true indeed; scarcely an hour ago I found Crabolus bragging to Herod's chief centurion about his battlefront experiences. I doubt he has ever lifted a sword in his life!"

"I know it! And yesterday, he was practically licking Herod's boots to try to get attention!"

Chuza snickered. "He also is bent on mischief and gossip. When he isn't flattering Herod to his face, he's grumbling about him to the other unhappy souls.

"I wish he'd just do his job. He was supposed to put a hundred more drinking vessels out tonight, but he didn't follow through on his orders. Servants used to serve with dignity and honor, not like this Crabolus. I don't trust the man to do anything right."

"Are you now also in charge of the servants?" Joanna asked, half-jokingly.

"I'm in charge of whatever Herod asks me to be," Chuza gritted, "and it's becoming a nuisance. On days like this, I wish I wasn't Herod's chief steward. How about Stephanus, have you seen him?" At that moment, Stephanus appeared from behind them.

"Hello there, my friend!" Stephanus greeted Chuza. "What a grand celebration!"

"I appreciate your cheerfulness," Chuza replied, "but I wish this would be over. I don't trust anyone, especially at a party like this. People get drunk, and start breaking things."

Stephanus nodded, "... and us stewards get blamed for everything."

Joanna nodded a friendly smile to Stephanus. She considered him a trusted friend.

"Are you keeping good care of my husband?" she said to Stephanus.

"I surely am, dear lady. I surely am." He smiled approvingly, tapping Chuza on the arm.

"Herod wants us to move those tables by the gate," Chuza directed Stephanus, "They serve no purpose, and are in people's way."

Stephanus nodded in agreement. "Perhaps to one of the side rooms for the moment? We can always return them once the party is finished."

"An excellent idea!"

Joanna listened to them, and admired the way they laid out their plans to get the work done. Stephanus is good for my Chuza, she reasoned, especially with raving Herod in charge. I would trust Stephanus with anything! Indeed, Stephanus had become Chuza's closest worker, and their relationship had become as much 'friend' as 'boss to subject.'

One time, after one of Herod's tantrums, the two of them had spent an hour or so laughing off Herod's charades. Laughter had always made the world a better place, at least for awhile. Such friendship brought on a degree of contentment, which helped Chuza go home more at ease.

Yes, she thought, A friend of Chuza's, is a friend of mine.

Stephanus reached for a parchment secured on the inside of his cloak. "Two vases were broken in the fist fight tonight, and another large Grecian floor pot was cracked by people jostling in the entrance."

Chuza chuckled, "Oh well, as you and I both know, Herod is not short for money. He can buy another with no problem."

"Yes, funds are increasing every week, a sizeable profit from last year."

"Thanks to us," chuckled Chuza.

Joanna had heard that topic a hundred times, and so, rather than engaging in conversation, she pretended to hear by nodding, but all the while making the occasional glance across the large group of men and women in the banquet hall. Had Chuza not been present, Joanna would have been approached by several men, and may have agreed to their pleasure. But she knew Chuza would soon be off to another one of Herod's tasks, and she would have her chance then.

Chuza proved to be loyal through and through, but his allegiance to Herod was obviously his paramount devotion.

Right then, Miriam, one of the servants walked past Joanna with a plate of olives, pomegranates, figs and other fruit. She smiled at Joanna, and stopped for a moment.

"Hello, Joanna!"

"Miriam!" Joanna exclaimed with a smile. "You are doing such a good job! And you are dressed so nicely tonight!"

Miriam was beaming at the compliments given by Joanna. "I've got to keep going; I can see Crabolus coming." And with that she quickly turned with her plate to serve some more people.

Joanna spotted Crabolus, head of the servants, for a moment, but he disappeared down another hallway.

Poor Miriam, Joanna thought, she's so sweet, and she has to put up with that man!

Another servant, Chaya, came up to the three-some. She greeted Joanna with a quick smile, and then looked at Chuza. "Herod needs you. There is a problem with the dignitaries. Something is wrong with their food."

Chuza and Stephanus were told Crabolus was in the middle of it all, and Chuza, being the wise peace maker, needed to look after the problem.

Chuza tilted his head and glanced at Joanna to indicate he was leaving, and he and Stephanus marched down through the crowd, continuing their conversation.

Joanna took a step forward, remembering the argument she had had with Chuza that morning.

"You're never here," she had said.

"There's too much to do," Chuza had retorted.

"You used to love me enough to..."

Chuza had broke in, "Enough to follow you around to every shop in town. But let me remind you—that was before Herod employed me. I can't help what Herod demands."

"All I'm saying is you've changed—and not for the good."

Chuza had been getting more agitated as their conversation went on, gathering his things in hand. He had offered a last comment over his shoulder as he walked out the door: "Things might be better if you gave me the same kind of attention you give the soldiers!"

Her face had turned an instant red with embarrassment and rage. "So that's what you think!" she had yelled after him.

"That's what he'll get then!" she had said to herself.

Sure enough, about ten minutes later, another soldier appeared beside her.

"Quite a party isn't it?" He was a bit shorter than the one tagged to Mary, but in similar attire, and equally attractive. She nodded and smiled.

He moved in front of her, and leaned back on the fence in order to inspect her closely, "Mary asked me to come."

"Mary..." she repeated with a wink, "She asked you to come here?"

"There's a party a short way down the hill. Better than this one... With common folk!"

"Hmmn..." she surveyed him. He had thick curly black hair, and a permanent boyish smile. "I suppose..."

"Come On! It'll be fun!"

"What's your name?"

"Ephraim. What's yours?"

Joanna tilted her head and stared him in the eye, "You were sent here by Mary, and she didn't tell you my name?"

"Alright, you caught me," he bowed at the waist, then backed up. Then he looked straight at her and said emphatically, "Joanna. My utmost apology. Allow me to begin again: Joanna—would you like to accompany me to a wonderful party in Tiberias?"

Joanna chuckled, and threw her hair back playfully. She glanced over in the direction Chuza had gone. The way was still clear. She turned toward Ephraim, and took his arm.

- - -

Over in the northern section of Tiberias, Joanna and Ephraim could hear the faint sound of flutes and lyre. At first they were only a trickle in the airwaves, with the hurried shuffle of their feet along the road broken by Ephraim's enthusiastic chatter. Unlike most Roman soldiers, he seemed more warm, and gentle. Most Romans were built like iron; strong, but cold. Ephraim, on the other hand, was warm. He kept glancing at Joanna as though he had won a prized possession. Now that Joanna was away from the peering eyes of the palace attendees, she enjoyed the attention.

The music grew louder, and Joanna soon realized it came from one of the larger homes in the area. She entered, and noted that, other than Mary's escort, the party was absent of any Roman dignitaries. It was certainly different to those she usually attended. She couldn't help notice other differences as well. Most Romans had images of Zeus, Pluto, or other recognizable gods on their walls.

Not here though. Neither was the home Jewish. Had it been Jewish, something to honor one of the patriarchs or ancient prophets would have been situated in a predominant place. Even the smell of the house was different than what she was used to. But she couldn't put a finger on it.

Anyway, Romans or Jews. It didn't matter. She would have a good time regardless of who was attending, she decided. She soon found Mary and the soldier, and the four of them engaged in laughing, eating, and dancing.

Chapter Two

The Tax Collectors

Chuza and his team worked feverishly to fulfill the spring tax quota. Each day, tax collectors from assigned areas arrived at Tiberias with their loot. They were immediately given more orders to fill collections on a new area mapped out for them.

Chuza had just reassigned such a tax collector when Herod appeared at his stewardship room.

"We're being robbed, Chuza!" Herod protested, "our own tax collectors are stealing money from under our noses!"

As Herod ranted on, Chuza got the picture. It seemed Herod had good reason for his concern. Several tax collectors had mismanaged taxation funds. Reports had confirmed it. Herod was sure the proper amounts were not being sent in.

"Let's get this straightened out, once and for all, Chuza. We have only one month to receive all the Galilean revenue. We must account for every shekel, and of course you must record everything before you place the funds in the underground vaults. Bring in the tax collectors at once!"

"But how shall the collectors do their job if I summon them to Tiberias?" Chuza asked.

"When I am through with them, they will work twice as hard, and twice as hard means no more laziness!"

"It shall be done as you say, Herod," Chuza promised. "We will be ready for the convoy from Rome."

Herod headed back to the entry of the room, but left a parting comment, "Rome demands their wealth, Chuza. We must be ready. But don't forget to keep our share. We don't want them extorting us!"

Chuza immediately summoned horsemen to speedily ride throughout the Galilean towns, and call the tax troops in. Chuza made arrangements for their hasty arrival, and scheduled an important meeting for all the tax collectors under his leadership.

Two days later, Chuza sat with all the tax collectors. No one dared defy Chuza's command. They all sat in a semi-circle in Herod's courtroom, facing the front. Chuza sat on his seat just off to the side of Herod's throne, awaiting Herod's grand entrance. Directly in front of Chuza sat Levi, son of Alphaeus, the very person whose activities were in question. Rumor had it that Levi threw a party in his home town of Capernaum for a number of tax collectors. He then tried to gain political favor by returning taxes to select people in the area.

Chuza held up his hand until the chatter of voices stilled, and was about to speak, when the familiar stomp of Herod's feet could be heard coming through the door. Everyone stood straight as he made his way with an angry scowl to the throne, and plopped down.

"Sit," he commanded everyone. Herod stared at the group before him, and Chuza had momentary flashbacks of previous meetings. In the same room, Herod had kicked and wrecked chairs; raved, stomped and yelled; and even punched his subjects over the smallest of misdeeds.

Now Herod stared straight at Levi. "What is this I hear of you, giving out tax gifts to people?" He leaned crookedly over the front of his throne as he often did, and continued without waiting for Levi to answer. "You are a leader of tax collectors! Is this the way you treat Herod? Is this the way you treat Rome? By using tax money to throw dinner parties with your friends? And most of all, you take the taxes belonging to me, and give them out to others? Who are you making wealthy with my taxes?" His voiced thundered through the courtroom, until at the end, he screamed, "Now tell me, what am I to make of this treachery?"

A number of chairs skidded a few inches on the stone floor, as several occupants readjusted their seats.

Levi stood to his feet. "Most honorable Herod Antipas," he said, "Please allow me to speak."

"Say on," Herod said, slumping back into his chair, exhausted.

"Four days ago, I was sitting in my taxation booth just outside Capernaum, when four men passed by, carrying a cot where lay another man, completely paralyzed. They were heading into town, and I asked them where they were going. They told me they were going to Capernaum to find a man, Jesus, of Nazareth, who was performing many amazing miracles there."

"I hope you are not going to tell me you gave the tax money to this 'Jesus' person," Herod snickered.

"No," Levi said, and then continued. "About two hours later, a large number of people came down the road. I could see right away it was the same four men. However, the paralyzed man was no longer confined to a cot. Instead, he walked and jumped, and appeared to be completely healed. I became convinced Jesus had done a miracle! Then Jesus passed by my small booth. He stopped and spoke directly to me, and asked me to be his follower."

"And you said?"

"Oh, noble Herod, I had no choice. My spirit compelled me to follow." Levi nervously stuttered as he continued, "The next... next day, I wanted so much for my colleagues to meet Jesus. I invited Him to my home as my special guest, and also invited several other tax collectors as well, so they could meet Him."

Herod spat on the floor, stood up and leaned disgustedly on the side of his throne, "I don't care a bit about this Jesus. Tell me about the tax money."

"Yes. Please have patience with me, King Herod. It was at this gathering where I announced my intentions. You see, previous to this I often took in more taxes than what the law required. People hated me because I cheated them. I am ashamed to admit that I took extra money from people, and kept it for myself."

Herod stopped him, "You need not tell me about keeping tax money. I am well aware of this practice. However, you took the regular portion of what belongs to me, and kept it for yourself."

He continued, "No, king. I kept none of the regular portion. This report is not true, oh Herod. I would never give funds to others for political gain, for my allegiance is to you. I gave of my wealth to the poor, and only gave them from the funds I had received through dishonest gain, not from the taxes marked for you, king Herod."

"Who else attended Levi's party?" Herod wanted to know, "Show me your hand."

About a dozen men lifted their hands. Herod paced back and forth across the floor. He restrained himself, which was quite unusual, but he also understood the value of these men to the economy of the palace. He bit his lower lip. He himself was guilty of over-taxing. But he also knew he had to make a point, and in keeping with his usual bullying practices, he sought out the smallest member of the tax group.

"You there…" he pointed at an extremely short man, almost hidden by the others in front, "Your name is… Dimenius. Is that correct?"

A beady head and short torso appeared from no where and leaned around the person sitting in front of him, "Yes I am Dimenius from Bethsaida."

"Are you also part of this group of friends?" Herod inquired.

"Yes, and I used to charge above the required taxes for my own profit. But I gave money back to those I cheated, and much of it to the poor because I cannot remember who I stole from."

"And of course I am impelled to ask of you—Why this change from thief to being so liberal with Caesar's money?"

"My brother, who lives in Jericho, was the first member of my family to become a disciple of Jesus. He told me about this man Jesus, who speaks and lives truth, and challenges all who would follow to be people of truth too."

"Your brother is also a tax collector?" Herod wrinkled his eyebrows in unbelief. "What is his name?"

"Zacchaeus," stated Dimenius.

Herod laughed, staring at his little bald head. "Indeed! I have met that man. Yes... from Jericho as you say, in Pilate's jurisdiction. He looks like your twin!"

Luke 19: 1 Jesus entered Jericho and was passing through. 2 A man was there by the name of Zacchaeus; he was a chief tax collector and was wealthy. 3 He wanted to see who Jesus was, but being a short man he could not, because of the crowd. 4 So he ran ahead and climbed a sycamore-fig tree to see him, since Jesus was coming that way.

"He is a small man as I am, and now, since becoming a follower of Jesus, he is an honest one. We now both know stealing is wrong. Over the years I collected a lot of wealth in that way, but recently I have sold much of my goods, and given my wealth to the poor. But I did not take any of your money, Herod."

Herod smiled crookedly, "This Jesus seems to be a favorite hero of my tax collectors. Maybe someday I will meet him myself," He laughed. Herod looked over at Chuza, laughing. "We certainly have picked an idiotic group of tax collectors, haven't we!"

Chuza managed a brief smile, still not sure what Herod would do next.

However, it seemed Herod decided no real harm had been done, and promptly dismissed the entire group. "OK, let's get on with the real business, men. Get those taxes in here, and not so many parties! Especially you, Levi and Dimenius! Now get out of my sight!"

Joanna

The crowd quickly disassembled without a word, surprised that no one was beaten or arrested.

Chapter Three

The Parthian

As Joanna and Mary shuffled over the last hill, the muted outline of a fishing village etched a dark grey silhouette against the lighter grey sky. In the evening mist, various homes collected awkwardly on the side of a gentle slope.

"There's Magdala," Mary said, as she had done on a hundred trips before.

Mary's house blended in with many of the white stone homes with rounded roof line, but with one difference. A stone wall bordered the large yard and the unmistakable metal mallet gate gave it a sense of elegance and security. Joanna was the closest and only true friend who entered the premises. That wasn't to say others didn't visit the home, but for a different reason. Mary brought her male guests here on frequent occasions.

All Mary's neighbors knew about her encounters, too. They talked among themselves, glancing once and awhile at Mary's house with an air of haughty disdain. Mary, however, flitted about with no concern for what people thought. She owned her life, and planned to live it to the fullest!

Now Joanna and Mary marched through the gate and towards the house. Mary spotted a small stone box on a table beside the door.

"Hey, someone left me a gift!" she said, and smiled.

She opened the lid, and a strong but beautiful fragrance flooded the air. She replaced the lid and carried the box inside, along with the attached papyrus note. Moving to a simple wooden chair, Mary sat cross-legged and began to read the letter to herself.

"Let me see," begged Joanna.

"No, not yet," laughed Mary as she shielded the note with her arm, "I must review the contents before I can risk letting someone of your nobility read it."

"So my friendship is not as important as my nobility!" Joanna joked, "and I thought we had a friendship relationship, not one of nobility to peasant!"

"Contrary, my dear friend. You, being a steward's wife, means little to me. I do enjoy Herod's parties, though. If it wasn't for you, I'd have to stick to the common people's parties!"

Joanna laughed.

"Joanna," Mary said, ignoring the previous comments, "You make too much of these notes. They are meaningless comments from men... from men who come and go." Mary wrinkled her face in indifference, "And to be truthful, the parties are more beneficial to my sense of adventure than any life-long purpose. This is merely... entertainment!" She gestured a casual open hand toward the note before her. "Now, will you let me read the rest of this?" With that she let out an occasional "oooh" and "mmm," and finally purred, "this guy is definitely romantic!"

"What does it say?" Joanna asked.

"He says I am a 'perky parakeet!'" Mary snickered at the thought of being compared to a bird, but enjoyed the attention she had gained from this man, "...and I am like nectar to a honey bee! He certainly is the romance king of all men!"

They both chuckled. "Yes, but don't they all seem so complimentary!"

Mary smiled. She thought about the many such encounters she had, most of which had ended with little more than a memory.

Joanna had been present for several "doubles" as they called them. Mostly military men, disciplined on the battle field, but human animals off the field, driven by their selfish urges, uncaring about who or what got in their way. Most of them were drunk, and didn't even know where they were. They, no doubt, had little recollection of the encounters themselves.

"We have to take these lovers for what they are, and no more," Joanna said. "True love runs deeper than what takes place with a man and a woman when she is too lonely to say no. But for me... Life always points me back to the adventuresome, yes even the daring, and the risk of having Chuza catch me in an act of betrayal."

"You take too many chances," Mary interjected, "but I don't have that problem. No husband here! See, I'm free as a bird!" Mary spread her arms and twirled twice in a quick 'bird dance' in the middle of the floor.

"Parakeet!" Joanna yelled. They both laughed.

"Who is the note from?"

"There's no signature, but I have an idea who..."

Mary stopped again to study the note she had received, unaware that Joanna had become pensive, and withdrawn.

Joanna took slow deliberate steps across the stone floor and stopped, but Mary continued to study her note.

Joanna peered at an invisible spot on the floor beside her as she continued. "I feel so empty sometimes—so unloved and unfulfilled in love. Life is like a hollow ram's horn which plays for a while, then clatters as it is set down on a table. I wish my life was more fulfilling."

She lifted her head to gain a response from Mary, but realized Mary was still engrossed in her own world.

"Mary," Joanna spoke louder to get her attention.

Mary lifted her eyes, wondering at Joanna's urgent tone.

"Mary," Joanna repeated, "When I receive a love note, I can't say I feel better... maybe at the time... but the good feelings don't last.

"Sometimes we get an invitation to a grand party. 'This party,' they say, 'is going to be the best, better than all the rest'—and we get all excited about it. But after the party is over, we go back to the same boring life..."

Joanna, for a moment, looked straight in the eyes of her close friend. Never before had she allowed herself to be so real—so vulnerable. She gazed back at the floor. Before, when they talked, they laughed, they made plans, and discussed the excitement of past encounters. But now Joanna laid out her empty heart with a greater transparency. She had let her guard down, and she had no idea what Mary's reaction would be. As she lifted her eyes from the floor, Mary's gaze met hers. Mary's mouth opened in mild shock. Joanna shifted nervously to the other foot, and waited.

At first, Mary didn't say anything. The lamp flickered impatiently as Mary stood up and placed a hand on Joanna's elbow. "Are you alright?"

A tear appeared on Joanna's cheek. Mary wanted to take her friend in her arms, but Joanna shrugged her shoulders back. With a quick wipe across her face, she stated rather matter-of-factly, "Alright? Yes, I'll be O.K."

Mary stroked Joanna's forearm, "Now, Joanna, sometimes talking helps...."

Joanna didn't smile. "Thanks, Mary, but like I said. I'll be O.K."

She turned and sat on a chair near her bed on the far side of the room. Joanna didn't feel like talking, so Mary didn't. The lamp flickered again as the last of the oil burned in its wick.

The next morning, Joanna heard Mary stirring in the other room as daylight began to illuminate the room through the window next to the bed. She stretched out of bed, and walked across the room to the cooking room. The parchment Mary had received the night before still lay on the corner of the table. Joanna took a quick look at it, and stopped in her tracks. What she set her eyes on shocked her, not because of its content, but because of the manner of handwriting itself.

"What's this?" Joanna said, startled. "What kind of writing is this? Look here—words are replaced with pictures in several places! This isn't from anyone around here. The writing contains the same alphabet as Aramaic, but it's not. I've seen this kind of writing before. It's Parthian!"

Mary came through the doorway, and stated in a matter-of-fact way, "So what?"

"'So what?' you say! Mary, this note is from a Parthian, an enemy of Rome!" Joanna almost yelled.

Mary headed for the food storage bin in the corner, but turned to look back at Joanna, "I don't care. Parthians, Romans, Jews. They're all the same to me. And besides, don't you understand that, when the Parthians gain power, the people won't be taxed anymore?"

Joanna gasped in shock. "Well, if you wanted to make a difference in the world, I'd think you would conduct yourself in a more reasonable manner than sleeping with the enemy!"

"Just because he's not Roman, you think he's the enemy. Don't forget you're not a Roman either, Joanna. You are a citizen of Israel."

Joanna bit her lip. Yes, she remembered how Herod had taken her and Chuza as Jews, and offered him a position at the palace. He had needed Jews to buffer the antagonism people had towards Rome. Secondly, he was making a good gesture toward many Jews who encountered economic difficulty. So perhaps it could be argued that Chuza and she were recipients of Herod's good will; that working for him provided a generous income. On the other side of things, even though most Jews had to 'lick the boots' of Roman authorities, they remained loyal to Israel.

"Yes, Mary. We are both citizens of Israel. Working for Rome is one thing, but honestly, did you have to choose a Parthian?"

"They're not so bad. They're good honest people offering a better way for us... if people would support them."

"I don't think you're right. Time will tell."

About two hours later a man knocked at the gate. He waited as Mary ventured out the door, unlocked the gate, and invited him inside.

Joanna gasped! Ephraim!

"I wanted this to be a surprise," Mary laughed, "After the other night in Tiberias, I thought you might want to see him again!"

"Ephraim!" Joanna stuttered, "How... how nice for you to come. I wasn't expecting to visit with you so soon!" Joanna didn't know what else to say.

Mary continued, "...and he is wanting to purchase some equipment in Tiberias tomorrow."

Joanna became rigid as she realized what she had overlooked. Ephraim had coarse black hair and a chiseled chin. She had seen men with those characteristics many times before, on the roads and in the towns. They had a few similarities, but were not Romans at all. Now she understood. The one who had invited her to the party in Tiberias was not even a Roman. He had worn the uniform of a Roman soldier, but he was not a Roman soldier. He was Parthian!

Her knees shook for a moment, understanding the impact of what had happened. She couldn't confront him about disguising his identity now, and she couldn't talk to Mary in front of him either.

Joanna scanned the man. Before, she had seen him in the shadows of night, and the subdued lighting at the party. Now, in broad daylight, he didn't appear much different than the average Roman, a fact which surprised her. However, it was the hair and the chin that were different. She realized another horrifying fact. She had spent the night with a Parthian, someone she always had been told to hate, and for good reason, too. Rome and Parthia had been at war for years. And now here he was again, right in front of her in Mary's home.

"Hello again," Ephraim said, smiling, "I must admit. Mary told me you were coming to Magdala.

"Did you figure out who sent you the gift?" Ephraim glanced at the box open on the table.

"Namen?" Mary figured she guessed right because Ephraim stood nodding at her. "Namen! I should have known. Is he still in Tiberias?"

"Yes, after the party, he had some business to do." Ephraim turned to Joanna, "I hope you don't mind me showing up."

"Uhh, No! Not at all!" Joanna blushed at her own stuttering, and tried in vain to come back with something sensible. Instead, she blurted, "You're not a Roman soldier, are you?" Joanna groaned within the moment she said it. Oh, my mouth! I'm in for trouble now!

The man seemed to take her comment in stride with an obvious lie, "No, not at all. Herod invited me to attend the party at the palace. He is extending a hand of peace to sojourners in the land. Even Jews are befriended by Herod these days!"

"Really? You're not a Jew."

"No I'm not. You are!" the man ventured, still smiling at his own wit.

"But you are a Parthian. I can't believe Herod taking well to a Parthian," Joanna persisted.

"Perhaps I overstated Herod's welcome," Ephraim nodded and laughed, "Anyway, I attended the party, and nobody asked how I got there!"

Joanna shook her head, "Unbelievable!" She turned to Mary, "Mary, did you know that Ephraim was Parthian?"

"Sure, Joanna. Namen too. I even had something to do with getting them there! That Roman costume didn't come from another land, you know!"

"Mary! You can't be taking soldier's uniforms and handing them out to just anyone!" Joanna exclaimed.

Ephraim interjected, "You must understand when I wore the Roman uniform, I was humbled; no... dreadfully disgraced! You told me I looked handsome, but honestly... For me it was simply a matter of necessity."

Joanna had no idea what he was talking about when he said "matter of necessity," but dismissed it as nothing.

"I have witnessed most Galileans living in awful conditions," Ephraim started. "In fact, just the other day I talked to a fisherman in Caesarea who is paying almost half his income to Herod's henchmen. As a result, his family can't even afford to purchase oil and flour to make bread!"

Joanna was about to speak, when Ephraim cut her off and continued his ranting about taxation.

"I remember about a month ago, I met this man begging beside the road just out of town here. He had been a stone and brick builder, but his business fell to nothing at the hand of Herod. With so much taxation, he couldn't even buy the tools he needed to continue. So there he was, right over there, begging," the man gestured to the north where the road led out of Magdala, "calling out to me as I passed by. So sad, so sad..."

"Oh, beggars are everywhere," Joanna replied, "and there will always be people disenfranchised with the existing government. If you took away the taxes, they would all waste their money on something else."

"No, Joanna, they don't waste their money because they don't have any money to waste!"

"You know we wouldn't have decent roads, or any conveniences without taxes."

"Taxes destroy the people!" Ephraim insisted.

Over the next hour, Joanna listened as Ephraim and Mary discussed the perceived awful plight of living in Galilee. Joanna agreed with too many of their arguments, so said nothing.

Another hour went by, and Mary and Ephraim still talked about taxes, and about Namen. Joanna stared out the window, dazed by Mary's connection with this Parthian. She began to consider going home.

"I guess I should be leaving soon," Joanna muttered, thinking how ridiculous it sounded, since she had arrived only the day before.

Mary excitedly stated, "Oh, wonderful! You can escort Ephraim to Tiberias."

Joanna felt a knot in her throat.

"Is that alright with you?" Mary looked at Joanna.

"Umm. Sure. I suppose..." If it had been a request from anyone other than Mary, she surely would have said no, but friends are friends, and Mary was still the best. And Mary will always be my best friend! Joanna thought to herself.

"Yes, that's perfect! Can he stay in the guest house? You know, the place where I often stay?"

"Why not?" Joanna said, all the while thinking of a hundred reasons why he shouldn't stay there. "Just to be clear, I'm going straight home." Joanna raised her voice slightly, to make sure Ephraim heard. It was important to clarify any false expectations he might have.

Joanna and Ephraim headed up the slope toward Tiberias. Ephraim tried to make conversation with Joanna, but she wasn't interested in talking politics. She had to remember that this man was still little more than a stranger. At least it was Ephraim, and not Namen. Escorting Namen would have been extremely uncomfortable, and she didn't need her best friend getting jealous over little suspicions. She reasoned with herself, Well, anyway, I'm not going to be in any long term relationship with a Parthian! Besides, I'm married!

Joanna couldn't help notice that Ephraim was bent on pushing things. He walked uncomfortably close to Joanna. Joanna made an uncomfortable cough, then stopped to re-latch her sandal momentarily. But Ephraim seemed unrelenting.

What happened next took Joanna completely by surprise. She thought she had made her intentions clear earlier, but Ephraim obviously didn't get the message. His hand touched hers, casually at first, but the next time, with unavoidable intent, and grasped her fingers in his. Then, in a swift motion, he grabbed her arm with one hand, and grasped her other shoulder with his other hand. He tried to haul her off the path behind a large boulder, but Joanna instantly dropped down, and scrambled, hands and knees, across the path.

For a moment, Joanna was too stunned to know what to do, but she faced Ephraim defiantly, puffing for air. She crouched low, scooping up several stones in her hand, and snarled at Ephraim like a cat with its teeth bared.

"Stay back! Get away from me!"

Joanna remembered that Roman men often took advantage of women they chose, but Ephraim was Parthian, and that changed everything. Had he been Roman, Joanna wouldn't have had any voice, legal power, and it wouldn't matter who the man might be. In court, the man would be excused, and she, a woman, would be convicted of adultery. And the punishment for the crime was death by stoning. But the fact that Ephraim now stood speechless and even backed up a couple of steps, pointed to the fact that he dare not take any further risk. If another traveler passed by, his true identity would be discovered. And it would not sit well for him, a Parthian, in a Roman court.

Ephraim stomped his feet, turned on the path, and proceeded to hurry along the path, leaving Joanna to catch up. Once Joanna drew near enough to hear, he turned his head back to speak, pretending not to be embarrassed in any way, "You're lucky I caught you when you stumbled back there. You surely would have fallen and hurt yourself."

Joanna managed a disgusted, "Hmmph!" then a few moments later she whispered to herself, "What an idiot!"

Joanna regretted going to the party a week ago, and regretted agreeing to walk this man to Tiberias. Mary was her best friend, but sometimes even best friends had to say no, and this should have been one of those times. A Parthian! she repeated in her mind disgustedly.

Now as they neared Tiberias, Joanna slowed to walk behind him rather than beside him. Even if she had been attracted to this man, she knew better than to be seen in public together. Such mischief would not be judged lightly by any Jews, and though Jews were few in number in Tiberias, the few were devout. She didn't need Jewish eyes judging her. And she dared not even think of what Chuza would do if he found out.

She almost told Ephraim to find another place to stay, but changed her mind. First, she feared what Ephraim might do in retaliation; and secondly, she had told Mary he could stay there, and she wouldn't break her promise. Why did I ever promise to do something so idiotic? she thought to herself.

Despite her frustration and anger toward Ephraim, she followed through with the most obvious plan, and offered him the palace guest house to stay in overnight, which he readily agreed to. She slipped him the key for entrance, pointed to the house as they passed by, and continued down the street alone.

The whole trip to Magdala had been full of unpleasant surprises, and she needed some time to process each implication. She had never expected to have anything to do with Parthians, let alone sleep with one. And even though it was a short encounter, she suspected the days that lay ahead would be a complicated entanglement. Mary had been her best friend for a number of years, but now Mary was befriending Parthians, something which bothered Joanna more than a little. To complicate things even further, Joanna had no one to talk to about it. Mary was such a close friend, but one of only few. She didn't have other close friends to talk to, and she absolutely couldn't talk to Chuza about those men.

She put that thought behind her, and focused on the present plan. She walked down the street, then swerved off to a side street, and headed up the walk to a small, cut-stone house.

She reached out her knuckles to knock at the door when Crabolus appeared right out front of the home, on the street.

"What 're ya doing?" he grumbled, squinting at her through sinister eyes.

She turned red. "Crabolus! Caesar's nation! What are you doing, following me?" Joanna had observed far too much of his antics to trust him at all. The last thing she needed was for Chuza to find out about the Parthians.

"So Joanna! What were you doing with that man you were walking with?" He grinned from ear to ear, thinking he had caught her.

"Nothing!" she offered, which was mostly true that particular day.

"No, I think you were doing something alright! And I might just have to ask Chuza about it!"

"You wouldn't dare!" She made her way quickly to the street, fists clenched, not that she planned on using them.

"Well, let's say you owe me a favor. Maybe some inside preference to help me get a position with Herod's centurions. What do you think? Shall we trade? I keep this little secret, and you give Chuza and Herod a good word for me? I need that position!"

Joanna doubted her recommendation would mean much to Herod, but agreed anyway. She spoke the promise, but actually giving recommendation for this man — maybe not.

"OK, I'll give them a recommendation. Make sure you don't tell a soul about this."

Crabolus, now satisfied he had made a good deal, promptly hopped down the street, while Joanna slowly walked down the street, but not for long. As soon as Crabolus was out of sight, she turned back toward the same house. This time she knocked, and entered. Two hours later, the door opened once again, and Joanna came out, and headed home.

She entered her house to discover Chuza at home. Her heart stopped. He stood squarely in the middle of the room, staring at her.

"Where have you been?"

"Just got back from Magdala," she lied. She walked past Chuza and pretended to fix some dishes on the cupboard. Her hands trembled with nervous concern, and she didn't want Chuza to notice her reddened face.

"Crabolus said you were in town earlier," Chuza raised his eyebrows, "up in the north section."

"Oh, that'll be Martha, daughter of Thomias! She has the same black hair like me."

Chuza pondered her response for a moment.

"So that's it, then," Chuza concluded, leaving Joanna to guess if he actually believed her or not.

Chapter Four

Herod's Special Plans

Herod's mood changed faster than the neck of a householder's chicken. One moment he joked with the palace soldiers; the next, he kicked a bronze kettle down the stone corridor. The dozen or so palace reps pretended not to notice the clang of metal on stone. They ignored the deepening etches around Herod's eyes and brow. Instead, they looked away, and chattered to each other in lowered tones about daily business. From the corner of their eye, however, they kept a careful watch on the king, trying not to look alarmed, yet ready to scurry out the door should Herod antics escalate.

Chuza continued his conversation with Stephanus, giving the same kind of cautionary side-glances toward Herod. They discussed everything from safety around the stable, to taxation collection. At the present time, they planned the arrival of a special guest.

"Is everything prepared for Neodius when he comes?" Stephanus asked. "He will be here in a few days."

"Yes, and his family will also come, but later. Neodius will receive a royal escort from the borders of Seleucia. The captain of the guard is overseeing their trip. Ten days later, when his companions arrive, a special reception is to take place for him. The cooks and attendants will be ready."

Chuza lowered his voice, and continued, "I don't know why Herod got so upset a moment ago. Yesterday, he was quite enthused about the arrival of his guests. All he could talk about was the 'wonderful' Neodius."

Just then Crabolus came around the corner. He picked up on Chuza's last remark.

"Unfortunately," Crabolus added.

"What do you mean?" Chuza asked, trying to keep his nose from twisting in disdain.

Crabolus moved closer to Chuza and Stephanus, making sure he kept some distance between he and the other prominents in the palace. He tugged slyly on Chuza's sleeve, "Come with me."

Chuza and Stephanus followed him outside to the far corner of the court, where thick greenery sheltered part of the garden from view of the palace. Crabolus stopped and turned to the other two men. His hair was disheveled, and two broken teeth framed three more crooked ones that grew from his lower gums.

"I uncovered some information which may be of interest to you, my friend. Of course, I would only divulge this kind of—well, you could say, secretive thing, because I trust you."

"Yes?" replied Chuza, not sure if Crabolus was so much friend as he was mischief maker, "and now what did you do, that you don't want Herod to know?" Stephanus and Chuza both chuckled.

"It's not what I did, but what Herod is going to do," Crabolus chirped, "and you may be surprised, but almost everyone in the palace is in agreement with this proposal." Crabolus turned his bony head sideways, looking at the other two, and hoping for any sign of real interest.

Chuza turned to face Crabolus, not sure if "everyone in the palace" was more than Crabolus and his fiendish counterpart Justus. "If this proposal of yours is in such agreement, then why am I speaking to you here in the corner of the garden, rather than with the steward committee in front of Herod?"

Crabolus coughed nervously, "Wait till I tell you what Herod is doing, and you will agree that we must stop him—it is for the good of everyone."

Stephanus had already taken a couple of steps back toward the palace, and Chuza was about to follow, but Crabolus continued, "The servants are preparing for two parties. Within a fortnight, Herod will throw a second big party; this time for his step-daughter Salomis. He is inviting all the guards, the stewards, a large number of guests, and especially Neodius. I believe Herod has in mind to offer Neodius the hand of Salomis to marry next spring; at least that is what Herod's personal guard told me. This must be stopped."

"Crabolus, you are insane! You ought to keep your own opinions and trickeries to yourself and the silly little men who follow you," said Chuza with a slight smirk of disdain. Chuza did not care much to weigh his words with him. Crabolus was used to such insults, and didn't seem to even understand them. Fools don't listen to wisdom, Chuza reminded himself.

Crabolus went on, "If Neodius is allowed to become a member of Herod's family, we may all be at risk. Neodius has dominated all the common people of Seleucia, to the extent that people are moving out of Galilee in order to gain peace of mind."

"Oh, don't say another word, my dear Crabolus," Chuza said with disdain, "Do you really think Herod would allow someone else to dominate his own subjects?"

"Herod is an idiot," Crabolus blurted, "he doesn't even know who his subjects are."

"Whatever your puny brain thinks may be real to you, but leave me out," declared Chuza. He and Stephanus turned and walked back to the palace, chuckling to each other, leaving Crabolus to continue muttering to himself.

When Chuza returned to the palace, Herod was waiting for him.

"I wish to meet with you, Chuza, in a quarter hour,"

Chuza hurried to prepare himself for the meeting, wondering about the agenda. Perhaps Herod was going to drill him about a perceived lack of funding, or question him about where the tax collectors were at the moment, and if money was forthcoming. The session wouldn't likely be an angry confrontation; otherwise Herod would not have scheduled a meeting, but ranted and raved in the courtyard in front of everyone. As it was, Chuza looked forward to his one-on-one session in Herod's presence.

The porter ushered Chuza into the conference room. Much to his surprise, not only Herod, but six of his top centurions sat around the table accompanying him.

"Sit down," Herod spoke in a hard tone.

Beads of sweat appeared on Chuza's forehead, and he grasped the sides of his chair with a firm grip.

Herod cleared his dry throat and began, his raspy voice thickened with concern: "In the last week, two cities in Philip's jurisdiction in northern Galilee have given their allegiance to the Parthian empire." Herod furrowed his brow as he spoke. Chuza thought he detected a nervous shaking in Herod's fingers. Was it fear?

Herod continued, "The Parthian crusade is to win Galilee, one town at a time. As you know many of the country people have already listened to the Parthian lie, and some of them are defying Caesar's decrees for census and taxation. Worse yet, we believe they have been welcoming and supporting spies from Parthia or Syria. We may not even know who has defected to the Parthians. It is an immense problem."

"But they will not succeed," Chuza replied.

"Of course they will not succeed!" Herod raised his voice to a shout, "No one *has ever* succeeded against us, and no one *will ever* withstand the skill and power of Rome."

To accentuate the point, Herod picked up his gavel, and heaved it across the room, smashing it against the far wall. Both Chuza and the six centurions jumped.

Chuza hated these outbursts. Could not this man try to control himself just once? What an emotional tyrant! The actions of Herod made Chuza hate all Roman leaders, but yet he agreed with Herod. Rome was superior to Parthia, Syria, and Egypt in almost every way. They had faster armies, were more skilled, and had the strategies of a successful nation. While Chuza questioned the upperhanded control Rome maintained over all Galilee, he never questioned being loyal to the greater cause of Rome. If Rome was ever defeated, there would be so many factions fighting each other, national chaos would result, with massive bloodshed.

"Now," Herod continued, staring back and forth at the men across the table, "we will discover who is for us and who is against us." He leaned over the table as if to accentuate the point. "Is anyone among you a traitor?" His crooked nose sniffed the air like an animal locating its prey. "... who among the soldiers, the guards, the stewards, or servants is not in allegiance to Caesar?" For a moment he stared directly at Chuza. "What about you? Do you know who is creeping like a snake with the Parthians?"

Chuza shook his head quickly. He briefly thought about Crabolus, but dismissed it. He had already decided Crabolus to be a nuisance, but not a threat to Herod. "No one, oh king," he replied.

Once Herod had made his point, and even though unconvinced of everyone's innocence, he continued to the next stage of his inquisition: "Bring in the court attendants," he yelled at the porter.

A sizable group of attendants, both male and female shuffled in from the hallway where they had gathered, waiting for the summons from Herod. Chuza examined Crabolus as he walked in with the rest. He sure tries hard to get on Herod's good side, Chuza thought. They lined up along the side wall, several of them glancing at Herod's gavel which still lay on the floor at the back.

Herod repeated the throat-clearing habit, which sounded more like a growling animal, and continued in his usual raspy voice, "Now, I'm planning a gathering in honor of some special people. As you know, Neodius from Seleucia is coming with a few of their city's dignitaries.

"Most of you have already been given instructions on how to prepare for this exquisite event. However, you will come for another meeting tomorrow to be reminded of the protocol. Do you understand what you must prepare for?" At this point Herod checked with several attendants for their affirmation. "And," he continued, "there will be a special presentation to be made when his family arrives from Seleucia in fourteen days."

Crabolus winked at Chuza, who looked the other way, disgustedly.

"At that banquet, I will respond to Neodius' request for my daughter's hand in marriage."

Two of Herod's advisors jumped off their chairs, and leaning forward, one of them blurted, "Oh king. I have heard a number of bad reports about Neodius. Are you sure you want to..."

"Sit down!" Herod yelled, "How dare you question my decisions—especially family decisions! Beside, my wife Herodias is in complete agreement."

His mind was made up, and Herod proceeded to give instructions to the servants, butlers, and attendants on how to treat the guests when they arrived.

After dismissing the others, Herod gave direct orders to Chuza to take a generous amount of money, and proceed to pay for all the food and supplies that would be needed to tickle the fancies of the Seleucian group. "We must not spare one shekel," he said.

Chuza instantly realized Herod's request would require more than the use of regular resources. They no doubt would need to dip into the reserves for Caesar as well. Oh well, he thought to himself, we'll make it up with more taxes; we always do...

Chuza finally arrived at home after dark. For once, Joanna wasn't off in Magdala or some other place visiting friends. But he was exhausted. After finishing their evening meal, he slumped down on a couch, and looked across the large room to Joanna, now propped by her elbow on another couch. Had not Joanna opened a conversation, Chuza would have been just as content to sit and say nothing. However, Joanna wanted to get caught up on any of the latest news.

"So, how was your day?"

"A little unusual," said Chuza, keeping to his usual factual responses with little explanations.

"Unusual?"

"Herod called a meeting."

"What is he after now? More tax collections?"

Chuza began to summarize Herod's plans to entertain the group from Seleucia. "Apparently Neodius of Seleucia is making request to marry Herodias' daughter, Salomis."

Joanna sat up. "Salomis is getting married?" She remembered that Herod's wife, Herodias used to be the wife of Herod's brother Philip, in the northern jurisdiction. Herod had cheated on his brother by stealing his wife, and a fair bit of the wealth that came with her. The palace attendants thought Herodias to be quite demanding; the nation thought the whole scene laughable; and the Jews said it was "unlawful" for him to have his brother's wife.

Joanna was quite curious about the news and its implications. "Do you think Philip will be invited to the wedding? He is her father, isn't he?"

Chuza shrugged his shoulders. "I'm sure the Galileans will have the wedding all figured out—the way gossip spreads!"

"Oh! This will be big news! Can you imagine the pomp and procession at the palace? It will be an elegant and lovely event! Do you suppose Caesar himself will be attending?"

"I doubt it. He has nothing to gain from the marriage."

Chuza continued, "Oh, by the way, Herod thinks the Parthians are trying to take over Galilee, and he has the facts to back it up." Chuza laid out Herod's concerns about the invading Parthians, and especially his suspicions that someone might be betraying the Roman cause. "Did you know that every Parthian soldier must commit one robbery, and one hand to hand combat or sword fight to the death? It's part of their military training. The Parthian emperor demands they rob or kill someone before they receive their uniform."

"No, I didn't know... kind of ugly, don't you think?

"So have you heard of any traitors within the palace?" she continued.

"Nobody," he said.

Joanna's foot twitched nervously a time or two. She looked across the floor, meanwhile trying to think of any way to keep the conversation away from the Parthians.

"What about Crabolus?"

"Crabolus is an idiot!" Chuza declared without explaining.

Joanna got up to clean and put back some pots she had used when making the evening meal. Chuza searched through some parchments he had brought home. Laying them down on the table in front of him, he said, "You didn't stay in Magdala long. You must have been back by noon."

"Yes. No place like home... and besides, Mary was getting ready to leave for Capernaum," she lied.

"Did you see anyone else?" Chuza asked.

"No one."

Joanna turned in case her face appeared as flushed as she felt. What? Did he find out something about Ephraim? Had someone seen her and the Parthian on their way back to Tiberias? Was Chuza testing her out? To emphasize the point, she quickly repeated, "No, it was uneventful. Like I said, Mary's leaving for Capernaum tomorrow."

Chuza got up, moved to the next room, and got ready for bed. Joanna put the last of the kitchen ware away, and headed for bed as well. Both changed into their night garments, and she blew out the last lamp. Joanna slipped into one side of the bed, noting Chuza had already turned the other way. She curled her body lightly against his back, hoping for an embrace, but it never came. She moved a little to her side, took a deep breath, and closed her eyes. Eventually she managed to shake off all the mental struggles of the day, and fell asleep.

- - -

Herod's Mess Up

Even when things were normal, there wasn't anything normal about the way King Herod walked. A person might expect their king to have an air of noble elegance in their walk, but not so with this lumbering jackass of a man. He didn't make careful, purposeful strides, but shuffled along with his head down. His shoulders swayed from side to side as he walked, and his big, burly arms curled in a half-circle outward from his shoulders and then back toward his torso.

So it was on one particular day when the servants of the crown needed extra humor, Herod provided it in full measure. Many of the cleaning servants were washing down the corridor outside Herod's private quarters, when suddenly the door opened and out came the king. His right toe caught the edge of the door, and he fell, face-first outside the door. If that wasn't enough, at the very moment he tried to re-gain his balance, his shoe on the same foot came flying off, hitting the wall half-way up, and crashing into the oil lamp near the top. The lamp fell with a crash to the floor, hindered only by Herod's head on its way down, where it broke into a thousand pieces, and some of its contents flowed over Herod's head. In an instant, flames covered the back of Herod's head, and singed what little hair he had left.

Joanna just happened to be leaving Chuza's office when she heard the commotion, and followed the same course of others, who ran to watch, trying hard not to laugh, and avoiding direct eye contact with their ruler lest they would even crack the slightest smile.

Miriam and Chaya rushed to Joanna's side, peering at Herod from around and behind Joanna. Other servants also enjoyed the unfolding drama.

Herod grabbed a piece of cloth from one of the cleaners, and smothered the fire on his head. The thick greasy remains of the oil smeared down the side of his face, over his ear, and onto his luxurious robe. By this time Herod was so angry he took his burly arm, and swung at the oil dripping from his robe in disgust. But this was his greatest humiliation yet, in that his hand caught the opening on the side of the robe, and the entire robe tore away from his wrinkled body for a moment. The crowd gasped in shock, and turned their heads, but Herod yelled to them in embarrassment. "Get back to work! What are you looking at?" He continued to mutter obscenities to himself as he trudged back into his room, and slammed the door.

Everyone in the hallway buckled in gut-wrenching laughter, but quickly smothered it with their hands for fear of Herod.

Chapter Five

The Men in the Shadows

The next day, late in the afternoon, Chuza walked about the palace counting and recording the furniture. He whistled a song as he worked. None of the servants would be in his way, moving objects everywhere, straightening, cleaning, and changing things around. He counted the number of chairs and tables on the upper patio when he picked up on the sound of voices below in the courtyard. Chuza stopped his counting, and listened close. He was surprised anyone remained at the palace. Most of the attendants should have gone home by now, since it would soon be evening. The voices came from the lower patio. The area was almost a garden, with lots of shrubbery and trees spaced between a number of odd stone monuments boasting of previous military campaigns. The gardener kept this area in meticulous shape, but seldom did anyone ever spend time enjoying the beauty.

Chuza gazed down from above. Two men were huddled behind such a monument, and, in low tones, spoke to each other. Chuza tried to make them out, but only part of their heads and shoulders were visible. One was squarely built with wavy black hair which accentuated his leathery face and hooked nose. The other man who stood further in the shadow of the monument held a bronze complexion, the tell-tale color of a Samaritan. Chuza moved to a place hidden from view. Now the canopy of shrubs and trees below gave him cover. While he couldn't make out what they said, their whispers indicated they were engaged in something secret. Chuza ducked back every time the men checked upward. As Chuza peered from his vantage point, the men moved closer to the southeast corner of Herod's palace. Nobody dared walk too close to the privacy of Herod's quarters, but these two did. Something wasn't right.

Chuza stood in silence, nearly thirty cubits above ground level, and surveyed them through the visual protection of the tree leaves. His eyes followed them moving below, along the inner wall. Soon, the two men stopped to chat.

What are they doing? Chuza thought to himself. There's no entrance near that section.

Chuza knew the palace like no one else except Herod himself. Just inside those walls, Herod lived in his private quarters. Adjacent to him, soldiers utilized the dressing rooms, and next, were several underground storage rooms. Chuza almost called the soldiers, but calling them would have created quite a commotion. He decided, instead, to remain where he was; quiet, watching, and more than a little apprehensive. A full hour later, the two men left in the darkening shadows, and disappeared around the corner.

Chuza instantly headed down and questioned the guards.

"Oh, I think they are part of the group from Seleucia," one of them said, "Herod gave them special favors. He allows them to walk freely throughout the palace."

Chuza was perplexed. The group from Seleucia wouldn't arrive for another two weeks.

"You think they're from Seleucia? Who told you that?" he asked.

The guard answered, "I don't know." He looked at the guard next to him, "Do you know?"

The other guard shrugged his shoulders, "Must have been the captain." A third guard had another version, "A soldier came to me, who told me not to bother them because they were Herod's guests."

"I see," said Chuza, trying not to show his bewilderment. Something didn't ring true. If the group from Seleucia weren't expected for two weeks, then who were these men, and what were they doing within the security of the outer palace walls?

The palace guards hadn't helped a bit, so Chuza decided to do his own investigating. He walked out through the palace door, turned right, and followed the grey stone wall around to the backside of the palace. Something gnawed at him. He needed to find out why two strange men had been lurking about. It seemed more than mere coincidence that two of Herod's visitors would be in the courtyard so late in the evening. He scurried around the corner of the palace and stopped close to where the two men had been. Spots of flattened grass marked where the men had stood. He checked the ground for any clues why they had been there. He looked at the wall, first at eye level, then carefully examined the wall towering above him.

Nothing.

His eyes drifted downward and for an instant, he almost missed it. But inches above ground level, a small pile of hand-sized rocks, all edged for cutting or scraping had been piled for someone to use. A casual glance would have missed the stones, and Chuza spotted them purely by luck. He re-focused, examining the wall again.

"What?" he exclaimed out loud. To his disbelief, the mortar between four of the wall stones had been etched and scraped at. Chuza had no doubt the men planned to finish removing the stones and gain access to the palace. Judging by the damage already incurred, these men had been here at other times. Though they had not been successful in their attempt, it was only a matter of time...

Ten cubits further, the wall jogged outward for a short distance. The jog served two purposes: One, to strengthen the wall, and second, to provide access to the watchtower at the top. Inside each structure, steps wound their way from ground level all the way to the top. During times of war, the tower would be guarded day and night. However, in times of peace, it was just another place for a guard's regular check-stop each night. Chuza figured a guard would pass by at the start of each three-hour watch. He calculated if someone had spied the guards' routine, they would have up to three hours between check-stops to create mischief below.

Chuza stepped around the far corner of the tower. He continued his way along the exterior wall. But he took only two steps when he stopped in his tracks, aghast. Someone had not only attempted to remove several stones from the wall, but two of them had already been taken out! He peered through the opening. The hole led directly into the room where records and laws were kept. The opening was not large enough for a person to crawl through. Not yet! Chuza furrowed his brow. He'd find out what was going on. Tonight this area would have to be guarded. But how could he trust the guards? Judging by their response earlier, any one of them could be behind the treachery, or helping to cover for this infiltration of strangers.

He decided to find his trusted partner Stephanus, hoping he was still at the palace. His search didn't take long. Stephanus was busy in the accounting room.

Stephanus jumped as Chuza came into the room. "You know how to scare someone, Chuza! I'm recording today's receivings. These are busy days, and I've been staying late, with all the tax money and all."

Stephanus had coins piled across the table, and when Chuza came in, he sat before a large wrinkled scroll. He put his pen down, and rubbed his eyes.

"The work never ends," Stephanus said as he leaned back and stretched to greet Chuza.

Chuza broke into Stephanus' comments, "We need to talk. I just came from the courtyard. Someone has been trying to break through the wall right outside the law and records room downstairs. Did you notice the hole in the wall when you went for the recording scroll?"

"No, there's no hole in the wall. You're joking!"

"Absolutely not joking. Let's go take a look."

They locked the room, and headed toward the underground section. They were about to pass by the entrance to Herod's quarters when Herod came out and promptly asked them what was going on.

Even though Chuza realized Herod would be upset and alarmed, Chuza told him everything about the two men outside, and the hole in the wall.

"Guards!" Herod yelled, "I want four guards posted on each side of the outside wall tonight. No one is to be wandering around the palace unaccounted for, do you understand?" He poked at his captain of the guard, Plouton, "I want you to find out who told the other soldiers these men came from Seleucia. There are no guests from Seleucia here at the palace!"

Herod grabbed Chuza by the upper arm, and motioned for him to lead the way down the narrow stairs to the storage room.

"All the records and law books are in this room, Chuza. Security is of utmost importance."

Chuza nodded as they approached the room. They unlocked the room, and entered. With the help of a lamp, they began to search the wall for the place where two stones had been removed.

The block walls dotted with storage holes contained hundreds of scrolls, but none of them had been disturbed. Eventually they found a pile of mortar and stony debris on the floor. They shone the lamp upward, and found the hole. They could even feel the night air flowing in from the outer court. The guards who had rushed to their duties, were already outside, and their muffled voices drifted in.

Herod grimaced. "We'll fix this tomorrow in the light of full sun. I will get to the bottom of this."

He continued questioning Chuza, "Did you check the rest of the wall? Have any other places been damaged? What about outside my private quarters?"

"I am happy to tell you the entire wall has been searched by me personally. Other than the one place you saw, nothing else has been damaged."

"What about where the treasury is?" Herod persisted.

"I tell you the truth. There is no other breach. You can be assured your gold is safe."

Joanna

- - -

Meanwhile, Joanna finished up a shopping trip in downtown Tiberias. Merchants from Caesarea Philippi had stopped in Tiberias, with clothing from Italy, Egypt, and even beyond. She purchased two halugs of silk that draped gracefully over her shoulders and down below knee level. Along with the halug, she purchased both a leather belt and a metal belt. She admired the metal belt the most, which was ornately decorated with rubies and even a number of diamonds. As she turned to leave, she focused in on an ear ring and necklace set that complimented her attire beautifully. She couldn't resist buying them also. She proudly put them on and made her way to the palace to show Chuza.

Her new outfit brought the attention she expected, even before she reached Chuza. People glanced up from the yards as she passed by. She smiled with satisfaction. Wealth brought status, and she embraced her status with great elegance.

As she approached the palace gates, the men gathered there also noticed. Plouton, the captain of the guards, examined each person entering, but his examination of Joanna took on something more.

He was popular for a number of reasons. People admired him for his hard work. He also had a handsome physique to match, and women considered him to be a master at male chivalry. Joanna was quick to spot his not-so-subtle glances, and threw her head back playfully, strutting proudly toward the gate.

Plouton gave directions to the other guards, but didn't miss Joanna passing by. He stood centered in the middle of the gate and instead of moving politely out of the way, he waited for Joanna to draw near. Then he stumbled backwards a step at the very moment she passed. He bumped into her slightly and the other guards chuckled.

"Whoa, there!" Joanna giggled. She bent down to readjust her sandals. Her new ear rings and necklace dangled seductively from her neck. Plouton continued his discussion with the guards, but glanced a second time at Joanna, smiling coyly. Joanna ignored the glance, but couldn't ignore what they said.

"So we will guard the breached area in three hour shifts," Plouton directed, "and then you will be replaced by another guard. At no time is the wall ever to be unguarded."

A second guard asked about the size of the hole in the wall. Yet another wanted to know how long dinner breaks would be.

Joanna listened with interest. She discovered that everyone in the palace knew about the hole in the wall. She also found out Herod had made careful inquiry regarding the two men. However, in the end, none of the guards had given them permission to wander the premises. Herod had extracted some of the truth; the so-called 'permission' came from a man dressed in a soldier's uniform, but unknown to any of them. Herod reprimanded all the soldiers and guards, since they assumed too much. They all thought he was a new member of their rank under the direct command of Herod, not an unusual thing for Herod to do. Herod was both furious and fearful of the breach of security, and vowed that heads were going to roll. As Joanna listened, she heard the whole story.

So by the time Chuza arrived home later in the evening, she knew everything about the breach in the wall. She had her own idea that somehow Ephraim and Namen were involved, especially since Ephraim had masqueraded as a soldier at the earlier party. At any rate, she didn't dare say a word about them.

Chapter Six

The Jerusalem Connection

Tension in Herod's palace seemed to be increasing by the moment, and now the undercurrents were becoming unbearable. Maidservants, not able to stand the sight of the king, purposefully stayed out of his way. They huddled in corners and side rooms, guessing among themselves what sinister deed he was planning. With dozens of rumors flying about, they did their work in confusion and mistrust. In the stewards' sector, the tension was amplified.

Partly because they deal with that tyrant every day, mused Joanna to herself, and partly because of the pressure to give proper account to a man who could not account for himself. Every task seemed like a heavy burden, and every requirement seemed like a horrible nightmare. Herod's demands left all the stewards, including Chuza, in a grumpy, frustrated mood most of the time.

"I'm sending you to Jerusalem," Herod announced to Chuza.

Chuza was surprised, but he sighed with relief. Time away from the palace would be a welcome break. He would also take the opportunity to think about the prevailing questions in his own mind. Who had been behind the breached wall incident? Were the perpetrators really outsiders? Herod's earlier suspicions were likely more correct, and someone from within the Roman ranks was "sleeping with the Parthians" as Herod had put it.

Herod reached into a bag he often carried with him, withdrew a scroll, and handed it to Chuza.

"This task is urgent. You must take this sealed document and deliver it to Retinab in Jerusalem."

"What shall I tell him?"

"You shall tell him nothing. The scroll contains all the information he needs."

Chuza wrinkled his forehead. What was the connection between Herod and Retinab? Why was Retinab, a previous centurion in Herod's army, now stationed in Jerusalem, out of Herod's jurisdiction? And why was he, the chief steward, being sent to deliver the scroll instead of one of the new stewards? They were usually selected for such mundane errands of the king.

Herod continued to give Chuza the details. "Joanna is to accompany you to Jerusalem, and you are to leave tomorrow morning. I also want you stop at several towns on the way back, and collect funds from the tax collectors. I will give you a list."

When Chuza told Joanna the news, she wasn't at all pleased.

"I had plans to go to Magdala on my own," she pleaded.

"Sorry, Joanna. You have no choice in the matter. Herod specifically stated who was to go, and you are one of them."

Joanna shook her head in disgust and looked down. "Why?"

"I don't know. Herod has his reasons."

The next morning, Joanna reluctantly joined up with the servants, who had secured the horses, camels and donkeys from Herod's stables. They all gathered with Chuza and two guards who came out the gate near the most easterly tower.

Plouton stopped them as they passed by. "You are taking two of my guards. Where are you going?"

"Jerusalem. King Herod's orders," Chuza said as he rode past.

"Alright, then. Be safe on your trip."

They headed out for Jerusalem, a two-day trip. Joanna didn't smile as she mounted a horse, and followed the dusty road away from Tiberias. *Chuza might be pleased with getting out of town, but I'm not!* she almost said out loud.

She too had made plans, but not for the Jerusalem trip, and not including Chuza. Her plans would hopefully become reality the moment they returned from Jerusalem. She reviewed them in her mind as the reflecting waters of Galilee shrunk behind them into the horizon.

She would get together with Mary and then attend a party. The upcoming festivity was in Tiberias, just down the road from the palace, at one of Herod's friends. The other event, which she had not disclosed to anyone, but desired for many months, was to meet the captain of the guard, Plouton. Now that he had practically flirted with her, she enjoyed the thought of returning the favor;

and that thought had led her to imagine a whole host of impropriety.

She stared at the winding road heading away from Tiberias, and swallowed hard. Every step of her horse re-enforced the message in her head. It wasn't the direction she wanted to go. She couldn't think of even one reason to anticipate Jerusalem. She glanced at the two guards riding with them. At least we have some security, Joanna noted. She further appeased her frustration with the thought, Maybe Jerusalem will have some exotic shops.

Joanna glanced up at the two servants on camels. She comforted herself with their presence. They watched, ready to supply her with anything requested. She was thirsty, and with a simple gesture of her hand, they came immediately with a wineskin or water. Shortly thereafter, she needed her hair fixed to keep the wind from blowing it in her face. They immediately stopped and tended to her. But Chuza refused to keep stopping, which left Joanna and the others hurrying to catch up.

On the second day of their journey toward Jerusalem, they approached the river Jordan to water the camels and donkeys. The Jordan, with its luscious green banks, was lined with shrubs and trees, mostly untended, and mixed with dead-wood. The shrubbery was broken by occasional paths from people who visited the river. The smell of olive trees wafted across the small valley and past the travelers. The water of the Jordan, although murky, held a unique beauty of its own, punctuated by lily-pads with their white flowers floating on the water. The muddy shoreline held clusters of reeds here and there with cattails providing a perch for several blackbirds. They followed the river for some time when they observed a number of people who had gathered ahead at the river's edge.

"Uggh!" Joanna exclaimed to Chuza, "Look at the creepy man!" They stared at a bearded man who stood at the shore, speaking boldly, almost angrily to the crowd.

"You are a wicked generation!" they heard him yell, "Who will rescue you from the wrath of God?" The sound of his sermon was interrupted from time to time with the varied responses of cheering, mocking, and weeping from those whom he convinced to repent. But the man was relentless in his delivery. "You! You right there!" he pointed at a young man near the back of the group, "Did you not steal from your master yesterday? Repent! Fall on your knees if you want to escape God's judgment. Then, if you truly want to change your ways, come here and be baptized, confessing all your sin before God and these people!" The man ran full speed with obedience, stumbling over the grassy knolls, and threw himself into the water crying, "Save me!"

Looking towards the strange preacher, Chuza remarked to Joanna, "You don't suppose this is Jesus, the fellow whom Levi and Dimenius became friends with..."

"I doubt it. I understand Jesus is a carpenter's son. He wouldn't be dressed in animal skins. I have no idea who this is. He sure is strange!"

The bearded preacher continued. He wildly gestured with his arms and proceeded to call down the wrath of God upon the crowd before him. Chuza and Joanna kept their distance, wanting to hear and see out of curiosity, but certainly not willing to be part of his audience. The crudeness of the man's speech matched his apparel. He was dressed in the most unusual clothing Joanna had ever seen. A long garment of camel's hair was bound at the waist with leather girdle. His hair was long and unkempt.

"He looks like someone who crawled out of the Galilean desert!" Joanna crowed, "I wonder who desires to follow a man of such filth!"

Chuza stopped to get a better view across his left shoulder at the scene before him. "If he is a Galilean, I'd sure be surprised. Even the hill people dress better than that!"

"For sure," replied Joanna. She glanced briefly down over her own garment, the one she had purchased only the day before. It flowed gracefully over her figure, and was the perfect match for her smooth shiny black hair. She smiled, pleased with herself.

The man at the river took off his sandals, and waded out into the Jordan. One by one the people stepped out, and he took their hand and spoke to them. Then he took them by the shoulders, and dipped them under the water, and raised them up again. Most of those who underwent this exercise came up out of the water with their hands raised in celebration. Many of them danced in circles. They were ecstatic over their experience. However, neither Joanna nor Chuza wanted to understand or desire such a thing. "He is really weird," Joanna remarked.

Chuza looked behind him. A passing traveler was coming down the path. Chuza stopped him, asking, "Do you know who that man is?"

"Of course!" the stranger replied, "That's John... John the Baptist!"

"John the Baptist, you say! Yes, I guess his name would make sense," Chuza grinned thoughtfully, "I think I may have heard of him before."

"Isn't this the man whom Herod summons to discuss religion?" Joanna asked Chuza.

"Oh, yes! Herod has requested John the Baptist to come to Tiberias a number of times. He's been to the palace. I just didn't take the time to attend the speaker's forum." Chuza thanked the man for the information, and signaled to his servants to continue.

Joanna's thoughts drifted back to the purpose of their trip. "Herod didn't tell you anything about the letter you are delivering to Retinab?"

Chuza kicked his horse, urging her into a brisk walk, "He only said to give it into his hand, and not to his attendants."

"So Herod doesn't want anyone else to see the scroll except Retinab."

"Exactly."

Joanna continued, "Do you expect Retinab will discuss the contents with you, or perhaps write back to Herod?"

"How would I know?" Chuza retorted, giving his horse another kick of frustration. Changing the subject, Chuza informed Joanna of the extended nature of their trip: "By the way, since we have the guards with us, we are expected to make several stops on the way back to pick up tax revenue for Herod."

"Just like Herod to think of taxes!" Joanna scoffed.

Upon arriving in Jerusalem, Chuza, Joanna, and their attendants rode up to the palace entrance, where Retinab's servants made provisions for their entire party as well as the animals. Chuza was soon escorted in to Retinab, and Joanna was left to herself, and managed to make small talk with the guards at the gate.

A young man, unnoticed by everyone including Joanna, casually sauntered toward her. Joanna was surprised he did not pass by, but stopped directly in front of her. His small beady eyes stared straight at her. "I know who you are. You are Joanna."

"And who are you?" she demanded.

"You are a friend of Mary from Magdala, and also a man called Ephraim," he said, avoiding her question.

"I am not Ephraim's friend," she stated. She turned away momentarily, not knowing how to respond.

"...and I have a message for you."

"A message?"

He took her rather matter-of-factly by the arm. "Come this way." He led her away from the guards at the gate, and down to a few olive trees growing nearby.

Joanna examined him more closely. She hadn't noticed at first, but now she knew at least where he was from. The Parthian edge to the face and chin gave him away.

"I believe you are aware a movement is upon the land to finally bring freedom from Roman rule. This movement is growing every day, and we feel Tiberias is a pivotal city to bring ultimate freedom to the land. Your city is the place where people in bondage can begin to experience freedom. And I have something to offer you."

"Offer me?" she repeated, expecting to receive a gift, or a letter from him.

"Freedom. That is what I am offering you. You and your husband should join our movement. We can guarantee you a place of nobility in the land. Think of it! You would be like a queen in the land, instead of a slave to Herod."

Joanna was speechless. She never thought of herself as a slave, but before she could defend herself, the man continued.

"Look at you! You already look like a queen. Why not be a queen. You don't dress like a poor Galilean. You don't even appear like a dreadful Roman. This garment you are wearing is... lovely! I believe it is from another land... Maybe even from Parthia!"

"No it... It isn't from Parthia," she stuttered.

"It is lovely. You already have the fashion of a queen!" he flattered, "and you have so much to offer."

Just then, Chuza called out toward the gate, "Joanna! Where are you?"

Joanna whispered to the nameless man, "Chuza is a dedicated servant of Caesar. He wouldn't think of..."

"You might be surprised what people think when they are offered freedom," he said with a smile. With that he placed a small paper fragment into her hand, and said, "Don't forget me, now. I will await a visit from you tomorrow morning. Here is a map. Follow it, and you will find me."

Joanna lurched from his grasp, and jogged back to the gate where Chuza stood searching for her.

"I'm right here!" she called out, stuffing the parchment note into a small pocket in her halug.

"Where did you go to?"

"I was just admiring the beautiful trees in the grove. Did you see Retinab?"

"Yes, and I don't understand this trip at all. The message from Herod was only an invitation to Salome's party. Anyone could have delivered that message. Indeed, the scroll could have been sent by a regular runner."

"But don't forget you have to collect Herod's gold on this trip."

However, Chuza was furious, and not to be reasoned with. "Am I to be Herod's servant, running all over the country to simply collect tax money? Let the tax collectors bring their money in like they always do!"

Joanna asked further, "So Retinab had no letter to send back with you to Tiberias?"

"No, and he seemed quite surprised to see me with just an invitation to a party. It was almost laughable."

"That's ridiculous!" Joanna cried out, "Next time tell Herod to make the trip himself!"

"Of course, I will," Chuza said sarcastically.

"I think Herod's up to something!"

"...and it's not good," Chuza agreed. "Could be I'm replaced when I get back, you never know."

"Doubt that!" Joanna replied, "Herod knows you're a hard worker, and he's got to keep the money coming in!"

They made their way to Jerusalem's royal guesthouse, where an entourage of local cooks had prepared a special evening meal for them; roast lamb garnished with a number of tasty herbs and imported spices. A small group of musicians stopped by their table to serenade them. Retinab was present, but not for long. He made quick conversation, but seemed more interested in the affairs of Jerusalem than in entertaining his guests.

"You be careful with Herod, now! I wouldn't trust him too far!" Retinab remarked as he got up. Chuza nodded. With that, Chuza watched him turn the corner and disappear from the dining area.

"Once a centurion, always one I guess."

"Busy man..." Joanna nodded. "Just like you."

After their meal, they walked together to the Mount of Olives where they gazed across the open fields to the north, and the city of Jerusalem to the southwest. Joanna took Chuza's hand, and enjoyed the rare moment. It was a scarcity indeed, and Chuza didn't have to run anywhere.

"It's going to be even busier when I get back. I hope Stephanus finishes the inventory Herod asked for. If not, I'm going to be working day and night for a week!" It was obvious that Chuza could not keep his mind on anything but work, and Joanna frowned her displeasure.

She couldn't get her mind off something either. She had to decide whether or not to follow through with the proposed meeting with the Parthian.

"Do you meet with Retinab again tomorrow?"

"No, I'm done. We'll leave first thing after noon," Chuza pointed out as they turned and headed back. "First I must meet with Zacchaeus who is coming up from Jericho, and Matthias from here in Jerusalem. The guards will accompany me, and you can stay at the guest house while I take care of business."

That should make it easy for me to meet with the man if I want to, she thought to herself.

Chapter Seven

The Parthian Encounter

As usual, the streets of Jerusalem clattered with activity. Farmers drove their oxen through the streets. Lambs were ushered to the places of sacrifices. Money changers called out to the foreigners, appealing to their need of Roman currency.

Unnoticed by those rushing from place to place, Joanna shuffled down a narrow lane with two story buildings lined on both sides. As she walked, she checked the small note in her hand. Just a little further. She followed the lane, her black hair glistening in the morning sun, with a slight tinge of red reflecting from its sheen. Her cheeks shone with the bright Jerusalem sky. Her attractive face was graced with a long, slender nose. She strode with an air of confidence which hid her insecurities within. In contrast to her bold stride, she made a quick glance behind her every few steps. She had to be cautious. People might give unwanted attention to a woman walking by herself down the street. They might even take note of the door she entered.

A shop owner suddenly opened his door, and startled Joanna. He poked his head out, and peered up and down the street several times.

His neighbor from across the street called to him, "Did you get your shipment yet?" The shop owner shook his head, and, as he retreated into his building, he glanced Joanna's way. She also couldn't help see a young man, who leaned out of his second story window, and stared at her beauty. Is every man is town eyeing me? But Joanna reasoned Jerusalem was much too busy for that.

She neared the end of the block, and found the place. At street level, the small business appeared to be an inconspicuous leather shop. Within this shop, a man sat on a single stool, peeking out from time to time from between the lattice covering of his window. Joanna stopped and read a note tacked to the shop door which said, "Welcome Joanna." This fellow *is* bold! she thought to herself. She tore the note off the door, entered, and stood across from the man.

He was dressed in purple with brown stripes along his sleeves. Standing up, he planted his high leather boots on the floor, and faced Joanna. Her eyes almost popped at the sight of a single sheathe about his waist, which held an ornate bronze and iron sword. His tall hat, which he now removed, held several metal ensigns across the front. Slowly, he opened the front of his cloak to reveal an inner tunic where, across his chest, the name, "To the King's Service of Parthia" was embroidered.

He nodded politely, obviously pleased Joanna had come. Without so much as a smile, he motioned for her to sit across from him. He inquired, "Did you tell anyone you were coming here?"

Joanna shook her head no.

"Your husband Chuza?" he asked.

"He knows nothing about this. He is occupied with Herod's business."

A slight wrinkle appeared on his cheek, and he smiled when he said, "My name is Matus. I see you have decided to find freedom."

"Ah, you are a jester without an audience!" she smirked.

"But you are here today," he said, pleased with his success in convincing her to come. "You decided to pursue this opportunity further, yes?"

She tilted her head for a moment, then jutted her chin forward, propping it up on her fist. She didn't speak, but stared at him steadily.

"I need you to do something for me... Something which would expedite the Parthian way. We already know when Herod's guards go forth from the palace. It would really help to have the soldier's schedules. Even if you told me the times when the fewest soldiers are at the palace... Also, any special activities..."

He stopped to consider what he had said, and then continued as if to explain himself more fully, "...such as any future military missions..." He swept his hand across in front of him and towards the wall. "...times when the army is away. Yes—that would be very important for us if we are to accomplish our mission. We want to restore order to the land of Galilee as quickly as possible." He propped two fingers under his chin in calculation, and waited for Joanna's response.

Joanna looked up at him, "You are going ahead with the invasion, then?"

"Invasion! No!" He chuckled.

"Well, not exactly," Matus continued, standing straight once again, and moving across the room, "The Parthian cause is not an invasion. We are intending to send in a number of our top military men to infiltrate Herod's ranks. In fact we now have three individuals who have already done so. Indeed, they have gained Herod's trust. Really, this mission should not be very difficult at all."

Joanna questioned him. "Matus, why is it so important to you to gain power over Galilee?"

"It is not so important to me as it ought to be for you. Think of all the taxes that are being raised. Do you know where Herod's money goes?"

"Of course I do!" Joanna said, "My husband is chief steward. He keeps responsible account of every piece of money coming in."

"Are you not aware of how much ends up with Caesar in Rome? Only a small part of the funds stay in Galilee."

"Yes, I can guess that is true. The common people would be thrilled to have such high taxes removed. But are you prepared to make such changes?"

"Even if those taxes were not removed but just lowered slightly," Matus said with a scoff, "they would be thrilled, because we would be able to provide the kind of leadership that they would want."

Joanna understood more than what Matus had intended. The implications were clear. Matus was not as much concerned about the welfare of the average Galilean as he was interested in control, and the financial rewards which came with it.

As much as Herod was a dunce, perhaps she was one too. She shook her head, hardly believing she had replied to the Parthian's invitation. The two options were clear: Herod or the Parthians. She briefly thought of a third idea, one strongly held by the Jews. They believed a Messiah was coming to overthrow the Romans. Now that would be quite something! Joanna thought. Imagine having a Jewish king to rule over us... and over the Romans! But there is no Messiah, she reasoned, and if so, I would be too much a 'woman of the world' to qualify for His kingdom!

She dismissed the thought and refocused on the situation at hand. She remembered what Matus said would be her personal benefit if she cooperated with him. Who wouldn't want to be a queen? she laughed within. On a serious note, she calculated how fantastic it would be for Matus to be in charge instead of the raving maniac, Herod.

Just thinking about Herod's antics in the palace angered her, and she suspected some of Herod's attitudes had spilt over to Chuza at times. Although a kind and loving person for the most part, he seemed to be having increasing moments of frustration with life.

And it's all Herod's fault, the idiot! she thought to herself.

Matus brought out a small parchment from the bag on the table, and picked up a writing quill.

Oh! So this is why he wanted me to meet him here—so he could document information! The man began to lay out several parchments before Joanna. Matus first placed a map of the palace of Tiberias, complete with several entrances and hallways marked off. The other was a list of people's names.

"These are our key people who need to be standing ready for the day of liberation" Matus listed them off one by one:

"Albus"

"Gnaeus"

"Cicero. These three have already gained the trust of Herod."

He continued:

"Crabolus..."

Crabolus! I knew it! Joanna exclaimed in her mind. She tried her best to not show her surprise, and the man carried on;

"Blasius"

"Domitianus"

In the end, ten men were named. Joanna now remembered that Albus, who sometimes helped Chuza or Stephanus in counting money, had access to the treasury room. Albus could be dangerous, she decided. Joanna wanted to question Matus about the morality of what the Parthians were doing, but held her tongue. She was a woman. She understood the necessity for all women to accept the submissive path. She would simply do her job.

"I will send a messenger to you a few days prior to our big day. You will need to contact each one I have named, with the time and place to meet. Once you complete that, on liberation day, we will transport all the help needed to overthrow Herod, and bring order."

"Why am I your messenger girl?" Joanna asked.

Matus looked at her incredulously as he ushered her to the door, "You are a woman. Would Herod ever suspect a woman of insurrection?"

Chapter Eight

Returning to Some Awful News

Two days later, Chuza, Joanna and their weary attendants plodded up the last incline toward Tiberias. They had successfully picked up the taxation funds from several communities along the way, and couldn't wait to get back home. But they had no idea about a horrible tragedy until they reached the palace gate. All their friends and associates from the palace rushed over to them wailing.

"It's Stephanus!" they wept, "He's been killed!"

"No!" Chuza and Joanna exclaimed, "It's not possible. We saw him just before we left!"

"Executed!" they all cried, "Executed…. by Herod."

Even Chuza had tears come to his eyes as he thought about his best friend, now gone, killed at the hand of cruel Herod. "What… happened?" he made out.

"Herod said he committed tre-treason," they stuttered.

Chuza raged, "What! How can that be? I don't believe it!"

One of the guards put his hand gently on Chuza's shoulder, "I'm sorry to tell you Chuza, but it's true. Listen to me. Herod sent you to Jerusalem in order to find out who had been stealing from his coffers. He discovered money disappearing from the storehouse, and only you and Stephanus had access. So while you were in Jerusalem he investigated, and found a further loss of funds. It was Stephanus."

"Well that doesn't prove anything!" Chuza retorted, "It could have been Julius, or Albus, or even Petras. You know they investigated him as a youth for theft!"

The grief became too much for Chuza. He dropped to his knees, with Joanna also weeping over him, her hand on his arm. Chuza cried, "But why Stephanus? Oh, Stephanus!" Chuza looked blankly across the yard as though his friend still lived, "You could not have done this." He bent over until he collapsed to the ground on all fours, sobbing.

Chuza sobbed as he asked the servants to put the animals in the stalls. He took Joanna by the arm, and carried the tax money into the revenue room. He fixed his mind to avoid Herod at all costs, and hoped the king wasn't pacing the palace hallways.

Having completed the menial job of taxes, both Joanna and Chuza stumbled along the path to their home.

Chuza made the odd sniffle as he shuffled back and forth in the house. At one point he clenched his fists and leaned over the table motionless; his fists, still clenched, propped him up. Eventually, he dressed for bed, and soon fell into sleep, exhausted from the trip to Jerusalem, and deeply grieved by the loss of Stephanus.

Joanna, on the other hand, was in a real quandary. She knew Albus was the traitor. He was on the list of Matus' ten men. He had the key to the treasury room. The thief had to be him! She didn't know what to do. She hated Herod, and hated Albus, and hated Matus and all the Parthians. "I hate them all!" she whispered through clenched teeth.

Joanna couldn't run from the inner turmoil. Herod maybe had his problem with rage, but Joanna's was just as real. She sensed an unseen urge to escape—to find something, however immoral or unethical it might be. Only one feeling controlled her actions:

Restlessness.

Chuza, on the other hand, didn't even notice when Joanna didn't follow him to bed. He didn't stir the slightest when she quietly opened the door and slipped out into the night.

Joanna's discontent bore no logical sense. She was walking out the door, sidestepping the day of Chuza's tragedy. But something blocked out reason, and the same force nudged her through the open door and onward. The same inner voice supported her self-justification. She had sacrificed four days for Chuza, and now she needed to find her own source of pleasure.

In the dark of night, Joanna was merely a shadow, flowing along the streets, hardly perceptible to anyone who might be watching. Now that she had taken one step to follow the voice that haunted her, she found it easy to continue down the street. She focused only on the plan in her head and the craving in her soul.

She followed the street past the palace entrance and turned left at the next corner. She counted the homes on the east side of the street by looking at each lamp in the windows. Four homes later, she turned up the path to the door of a home with an indistinct lamp within. She walked up with determined effect, and knocked four times. The door opened a crack, and Joanna slid quickly inside.

Previously, Joanna had detected Plouton's flirtatious advances. He wanted to spend the night with her. However Plouton had an additional agenda in mind.

"Did you know I am the commander of the guards for Herod?"

"Yes, of course."

"As commander, I must approve all new guards for the palace. No one is appointed a position unless they are, first of all, interviewed by me, and have the seal of approval stamped by Herod.

"Approving guards is no problem for me, but in some situations, Herod won't provide his seal of approval."

"Seems to me anyone you approve, would be approved by Herod," she deducted.

Plouton coughed nervously for a moment, "Well, not quite. I have been in touch with a couple of your friends, who want me to approve other guards."

"My friends?"

"Yes. They are Ephraim and Namen. You are acquainted with them, I think."

"Oh, the Parthians!" Apparently the Parthians had been working on him as well. They would realize that Plouton had a special position with Herod, and that would be a definite asset to them.

Plouton cleared his throat again, "Since we're both in this together, I thought perhaps we might work something out."

"Like what?"

"I need to seal documents in order to get people approved."

"And Chuza has Herod's seal in his possession," she completed.

"Well... yes! I guess that's it!"

Joanna stumbled for words, realizing just how deep this problem with the Parthians was getting.

"They are paying you?" she ventured.

"Of course. But I am willing to share the wealth with you if you will seal some parchments for me..."

"How much?"

"Oh, let me think... How does ten thousand denarii sound to your ears?"

Joanna asked, "How much are Ephraim and Namen paying to get people approved in this way?"

"That, my dear Joanna, is a very private matter. I cannot tell you."

"Forty thousand?" Joanna fumed, thinking about the measly forty denarii she had received.

"Joanna, I cannot tell you. They told me I couldn't tell anyone."

"I'll think about it," Joanna replied, "and if I decide to help out, I want the money before you get the seals."

"Of course," Plouton smiled.

Two days later, Joanna visited Chuza in his office. As she greeted him, she couldn't help observe what was on the left side of Chuza's desk. It was Herod's seal.

Chuza's desk was covered with accounting documents. Each pile represented the account of a tax collector who had brought their funds to the palace. Behind Chuza, a large amount of shekels, denarii, and other currency was piled high on another table.

Chuza was accustomed to Joanna stopping by from time to time, and he would often get her to run an errand for him, or take a message to someone. Today he needed to ask Herod about something.

"Can you stay with my supplies here, while I just run over to talk to Herod?"

"Yes, I will." She peered at the seal on the desk as Chuza walked out the door and down the hall. She looked away, and then back at it again. If she was going to do this, she needed to do it now. Joanna walked to the doorway of the office and glanced both ways. The way was clear. She walked quickly back to the desk, and reached toward Herod's seal. She took it in her hand.

Suddenly she heard voices coming down the hallway!

Joanna pulled her hand back, dropping the seal sideways on the desk! It fell with a clatter.

Both Chuza and Herod entered the room.

"Greetings, Joanna," Herod said, hardly looking at her. He shuffled through the parchments, and pulled out two documents from the pile on the desk. Neither Herod nor Chuza noticed that the seal had been moved.

Joanna stood straight to recognize Herod. She raised her right arm to show respect, and waited for his greeting, but he was preoccupied with finding a particular document. She dropped her arm down, and backed up from the desk and area where they worked. Whew! That was close! she thought, and felt sweat appearing on her forehead.

Herod pulled two parchments to the corner of the desk, grabbed the seal from off the desk, and proceeded to stamp the documents!

"There. Send them off to King Caesar!" Herod announced.

Joanna excused herself. Sealing documents for Plouton would not work the way she had hoped. She wouldn't dare take the seal, and have them find it missing. She would have to bring documents here and seal them!

Chapter Nine

Confrontation with Crabolus

Joanna was still asleep at home as the light of dawn began to brighten over the Sea of Galilee. She didn't hear the wind blowing the trees surrounding her home, nor did she hear Chuza as he opened the door and left for the palace.

Now, the dull sound of the breeze outside deepened her sleep even further. The morning sun had already moved up from the horizon when a knock at the door caused her to jump. It was the wife of Crabolus.

"Is Chuza home?" she called.

Joanna rubbed her eyes and looked for Chuza.

"No, Chuza must be at the palace. You missed him. What do you want?" She swung her legs over the side of her bed, and moved toward the door.

"I wanted to leave a message for Chuza. Uhh... Can I give you a note from Crabolus?" The mistress scratched a note onto a thin layer of leather. She then rolled it into a scroll and handed it to Joanna. "Here... Will you take this to Chuza?"

Joanna nodded, and Crabolus' wife left as quickly as she had come.

She reasoned why Chuza had gotten up early. He was likely hard at work simply to get Stephanus off his mind. She couldn't help but share in the grief, and even feel sorry for Chuza, knowing what good friends he and Stephanus had been.

As soon as Joanna could freshen up and dress, she headed to the palace to find Chuza. On the way, she mused over Chuza's work and her life in general. *I have everything going for me, except peace of mind. My husband's work brings me great advantage. I have more than enough money to spend when I want. I have a degree of prestige, and I like the respectful nods people give me when I pass them by. But... peace of mind? No, contentment is indeed fleeting. Something must be missing. Why else would I obey such disgusting cravings every time something goes wrong in my life?*

She unlatched the brass closure on the steward's door and entered. Chuza sat sullenly at his desk, staring straight ahead. He only turned his head slightly to look at Joanna as she came across the room.

"Here's a note for you, my dear," she smiled. Chuza loosened the seal and unrolled the note and, having read the message, tucked it behind his belt.

"Who gave this to you?"

"The wife of Crabolus. She came by the house after you left this morning."

"No wonder," Chuza offered, "I can't imagine what he is up to now. He requests to meet with me at the fifth hour."

"What does he want?" Joanna asked. She was especially interested, knowing Crabolus was such a busy body.

"I will find out soon enough," he said. "Crabolus may be crafty in his dealings, but he's not hard to figure out. Just ask him the right questions, and he always comes undone. Too bad he doesn't grow up."

"Yes," answered Joanna, "and do some real work."

"Everybody complains about him. The other day some guests had to speak up. Crabolus served them with dirty cups and plates! He shouldn't be missing something so obvious."

"Bad work ruins the reputation of the palace."

"Absolutely!" Chuza agreed. "I'm surprised Herod doesn't have him removed."

"Perhaps Herod doesn't know," remarked Joanna, looking proudly at Chuza, "Herod doesn't call for sessions with Crabolus as he does with you."

"Remember Crabolus is only a servant. He may be a chief servant, but still, only a servant. Hopefully that's all he'll ever be." Chuza had also noticed a decline in the number of meetings between Crabolus and Herod. At least three weeks had gone by since Crabolus had been called to attend any matter in the king's presence.

"He could use more meetings... if it would do him any good! He's always either messing up, or seeking attention. Most people at the palace just wished he'd go away."

Chuza glanced up at the ceiling, and then brought his chin down into the crevice of his thumb and forefinger, squeezing it thoughtfully. He then clapped his hands together, and, pointing his finger straight ahead, he got up and declared, "This has to be done."

With that, he headed out the door, and turned down the hall, not in the direction of Crabolus' room, but towards Herod's private chambers.

Several hours later, Joanna walked down the same hallway, when Crabolus appeared around the corner. His face was red with rage. He grabbed Joanna by the arm and dragged her into the nearest room. Joanna almost lost her balance as he threw her through the doorway, and half way across the room, nearly landing on top of a small desk.

An angry scowl creased Crabolus' face as he spit on the floor.

"You swine!" He shouted, supposing a pig to be the worst possible comparison to use. "Why did you speak to him? Did you not realize you wrecked everything?" He stomped back and forth in the tiny room, the 'thud—thud' echoing each time his boot met the stone flooring. Veins stood out on his neck and forehead. His stubbled face was flushed in anger. Muscular arms swung wildly, with the threat of hitting anything that got in their way. "If it is not enough to wonder whether Herod hates me," Crabolus continued, "now you had to speak evil to Herod of me."

"I never..."

"I thought you and Chuza were my personal friends, but you are Herod's children." He pointed a bony finger at Joanna. "Swine! Swine! That is what you are!"

Joanna wasn't about to back down, and prepared for the fight. Crabolus was asking for it. She taunted, "Personal friend? Where do you get such an idea?"

"Well, you weren't a friend, and you aren't my friend!" Crabolus' remarks reminded her of children in the square, fighting over some little game they played. She guessed that Chuza had indeed complained to Herod about many of Crabolus' shortcomings, and Herod had laid into Crabolus in full measure. Somehow, Crabolus had gotten the idea Joanna was behind it all, and he continued to verbally assault her.

"You drove Retinab away from here, too, didn't you? If you hadn't accused him falsely, he would still have his position here!"

"Retinab?" she questioned, wide-eyed, "What does he have to do with anything? It was Retinab himself who requested to go to Jerusalem. His whole family lives there. Nobody drove him away from here!"

Joanna side-stepped in front of Crabolus, inching closer back to the door. "No one will believe I drove him away. Not me, not Chuza, not the soldiers, not the guards, not ANYONE BUT YOU — YOU CRAZY SUSPICIOUS FOOL!" she yelled the last words for emphasis. "Oh, you think Retinab was so sweet and kind, yes? Do you forget so quickly who it was that turned Herod against his first wife? Oh, yes — you know it!"

He turned a half circle and continued, knowing he was about to strike a personal blow. He curled his lips in mockery. "Joanna, of all ladies of esteem, you would know the goings-on of other men and their women!"

Crabolus turned to the wall, waiting to see if Joanna could create a response to his superb verbal assault. Instead, Joanna stood in the middle of the doorway. "You know nothing about anything, Crabolus — in fact, YOU are the swine!" She slammed the door behind her, but not before giving Crabolus one final look of disdain. The slap of the door against its frame reverberated throughout the court, but Joanna did not care. She ran between the shadows of the trees shading the path to her home.

Chapter Ten

Jesus, Man of Deliverance?

The hills of Galilee were covered with signs of spring. Yellow marigolds burst forth in the rays of the afternoon sun. At the base of the valleys, the sun barely reached the purple lilies as they waited for just the right hour to open their petals to the sky. Rocks jutted out from the tops of the hills, like random monuments erected on velvet grass. The panoramic scene duplicated itself on a hundred sunny days, except for one thing. Joanna wasn't watching the scenery. She peered down the hill at a multitude of people slowly moving along the hillside path more than a furlong away.

From her vantage point, she could see the main attraction; a certain man at the front and center of the throng. People jostled elbows with one another, prying their way to get closer to Him. Joanna moved down the hill and lowered herself on a large boulder, watching and listening. The event was chaotic; people yelled, shouted, cheered, and jeered all at the same time. The crowd was nearing. A group carrying a paralytic in their arms tried to get close to the man. Happy children chased each other in circles at the perimeter of the masses, occasionally interrupted by parents calling to them or scolding them for wandering off. A group of bearded men, Jewish leaders, wearing traditional long black robes, stood near the man, some taunting, others pointing and muttering to themselves. Close by, another group about a dozen strong seemed to be his private students, friends, or perhaps a security group. This must be Jesus, the prophet, Joanna decided. Everyone seemed to be talking about the 'great prophet', as they described him.

The crowd and its leader moved uncomfortably close to Joanna by this time. The mass of people confirmed Joanna's idea, as many called out, "Jesus!"

Suddenly a woman near Jesus shrieked and dropped to the ground. People scurried away from her. Without flinching, or even moving his foot, Jesus turned and pointed his finger toward her. The woman's body distorted and jerked in convulsive disorder. Joanna's heart pounded as she watched. She shook, scared beyond life, and sweat beads gathered on her forehead. She jumped off the boulder, and turned to run, but instead stood frozen in a combination of fear and curiosity.

The crowd, who now gathered in a large circle around the woman, peered at her as she writhed on the ground. Her knotted hair flung back and forth violently, and she tore at her scarlet clothing with her fingers until it was tattered. She curled her lips back and foam came from her mouth. Every few moments, she let out another blood curdling shriek.

Jesus was unnerved by the shrieking woman. Before dealing with her, he first spoke to the crowd, who now stood in stunned silence. In her curiosity, Joanna tried to make out what Jesus said, but only caught a few words.

"Lunatic!" Joanna spoke to herself. She was about to dismiss the whole scene as a horrible joke. She surveyed the crowd again. They still gazed at Jesus in awe. Joanna couldn't understand why they would want to follow such a man.

I'm not going any closer, for sure. I may be curious, but not that curious! Again Joanna started away, and again the crowd brought her attention back to the scene before her, as in unison they cried out, "Oh!"

Jesus took a step toward the woman, leaned over her, and touched the woman with his hand. She collapsed in a heap and lay on the ground, motionless.

What's going on? Joanna wondered. She viewed the scene from barely a quarter furlong away now. Jesus took the woman's hand, and lift her to her feet. The crowd went wild! Cheers erupted from every part of the multitude. Women and men alike danced for joy.

But not Joanna. She spit on the ground in disgust, turned and headed the other way.

Unknown to Joanna, Mary was in the crowd. As Joanna moved away from the crowd, Mary spotted her from the further down the mass of people, and came running to her.

"Joanna! What are you doing here?"

Joanna was embarrassed to be discovered in such a crowd. She opened her mouth, and said, "I didn't expect you would be here!"

"Neither did I. I just didn't think I'd find you anywhere near Jesus!"

"Believe me, it wasn't planned," Joanna clarified. "That man is Jesus, then?"

Mary nodded. "Did you see that woman over there?"

"Yes, a real lunatic!"

"I hear this sort of thing happens all the time with Jesus," Mary continued, excitedly. "They say these people are delivered from devils. A lot of people are healed too. Yesterday, He healed a boy with a broken arm. It was amazing!"

Joanna changed the subject, "You want to come to Tiberias?"

"Actually, I was thinking you'd like to come home with me…"

"To Magdala," Joanna completed, "Yes, I'd like that. I'm sick of the palace and everything connected to Herod."

Mary took one more glance at the crowd, then back to Joanna, and grabbed her by the arm, and said, "It's settled then. We're off the Magdala!"

They started northward across the prairie, and Joanna proceeded to tell her about all the recent events. "I had to go to Jerusalem with Chuza last week. I hated to miss the party, though."

"Wondered where you went!" Mary replied. "The party was wonderful! I think I'm taking a liking to Namen. Not like for serious future, but just… well… he's a real gentleman for sure!"

"Don't forget he's a Parthian."

"Joanna! Why do you hate the Parthians so much? It's Herod you should hate! Which reminds me, I had to pay taxes this week. On an income I don't have. But the tax collector said I had to pay what he called, 'base rate,' which everyone has to pay, whether they earn money or not."

"Oh, consider it, Mary!" Joanna argued, "You and I both know you earn an income. You just don't have a job!"

"Anyway my money should be my money, and not theirs to take. The Parthians wouldn't be taking my money!"

"Speaking of Parthians, do you recognize the name 'Matus?'"

"Oh, yes, Namen introduced him to me—he's a friend of his. Why?"

"He found me while I was in Jerusalem, and asked me a bunch of questions about the palace... Says he met you... he's friends with Namen and Ephraim too."

"Yes, Joanna. They are getting very serious about finding a way to remove Herod, and take control of Galilee."

"So I talked with him. I think it's a little scary how they are infiltrating the palace. But think about this: He said I'd be like a queen if the Parthians got in power!"

Joanna continued to fill her in on the various events of the trip, and also about the disastrous news of Stephanus death. "I can't believe it really happened. Stephanus wasn't a bad person."

Mary put her arm around Joanna as they walked. Mary continued, not knowing quite what to say, "Don't worry. Things will get better. You're so lucky to have Chuza."

Joanna started thinking about Mary's comment. Chuza was a good man. Perhaps she should do something to earn his attention. This would be a perfect opportunity to show him what a good wife she was. Chuza was sad enough with the passing of Stephanus. She would do something amazing, and in that moment she decided what it would be. Smiling at the thought, she carefully laid out the details of the plan in her mind. Chuza would love it!

They were just over halfway to Magdala when the unthinkable happened.

Joanna looked at the flowers, rocks, and bushes wherever she walked. But when something moved under a bush straight ahead, she stopped. She tried to warn Mary, but her voice balled up into a tight knot in her throat. The unmistakable flicker of a hand below the branches of the mulberry bush told her someone was hiding behind those branches. She grabbed Mary by the arm.

"What?" Mary asked. Joanna froze, speechless, but by the expression of her face, Mary knew there was trouble. They had been warned about the marauding bands of thieves along this road, but never encountered them. Joanna turned around to run, but another bandit stepped out from a bush behind them. Two more men surrounded them, and then it started.

One man swung a large branch which hit Joanna on the side of the head. Another tripped Mary and kneed her in the midsection. Two other men kicked them furiously, all the while watching the road for passersby.

Finally, Mary let out a piercing scream that stopped like a finger on the end of a flute when the bandit clamped his hand over her mouth.

"Shut up!" he yelled. The other man rummaged through their carrying bags for any money or valuables.

"Just take the bags," Joanna choked the words, "and leave us alone!"

Joanna thought about the considerable wealth in her bag. In a way, that saved the two from further injury. Had her bag been empty, she believed the men would have beaten them further. Maybe they would have even been killed. But thieves they were, and their main focus was to take and run—until one of them found a particular item in Joanna's bag. Joanna rolled her bloodied face over. They stared at a scroll with Herod's seal.

"Herod!" they kept saying to each other, "Herod!"

The leader of the group came to Joanna, and placed his boot squarely on her neck as she lay helpless on the ground. "You tell Herod and his soldiers, 'do not try to find us.' The next time, we will kill you!" He spit at Joanna through his broken yellowed teeth. "You will do this, won't you?" he increased pressure on her neck until she thought she would pass out.

"Yes, yes... Please!" Joanna cried.

As quickly as the bandits had appeared, they vanished over a small hill. Mary and Joanna got up in the middle of the path, and held each other in their arms, weeping. The ensuing silence was eerie, punctuated only by the sound of the wind rustling the long grass on the nearby hill.

"Let's get out of here!" they both said, almost simultaneously.

Mary and Joanna's frustration and anger raged all the way to Magdala. At least they had each other to lean on as they limped along. They cried together, and found some consolation in nursing each other's wounds.

It took longer than usual to reach Mary's home, where they tended to their injuries. Mary's knee was scraped and bloodied, and her body was marked with two swollen bruises, one on her upper arm, and the other on her back. She had received the one on her back when she tried to curl into a ball to protect her face.

Joanna's ankle was sprained, her nose was covered with crusty blood, and her face now displayed an enormous black eye. In addition, she still recognized the outline of the man's boot where he had pressed it against her neck.

Mary chuckled amid her sniffles, "I used to fight with my sister when I was little. We'd fight like two boys."

Joanna swabbed her nose softly with a warm wet cloth. She was happy to get cleaned up, but bitter about getting beaten up and robbed. Worst of all, the bandits had warned them to not tell Herod. This made no sense at all, for the moment Chuza would see her bruises, he would know something happened and would demand a full explanation. Herod had an uncanny way of finding out everything too, and he would be quick to deploy a search brigade to try to find the bandits.

Worst of all, rumors spread like wildfire at the palace. What Chuza knew, the guards would know, and what the guards knew, Crabolus would know, and what Crabolus knew, the whole world would know.

Mary and Joanna changed into clean clothes, and proceeded to get things back to normal. Mary hobbled over to the stove, preparing a hot herb cider drink. She stroked the front of her new dress downward, and sat down with Joanna at the table.

"How is your knee?" Joanna asked.

"Still hurts. But at least I don't look like a wounded goat. Your ankle?"

"Going to take a while. Maybe I can make it to Tiberias in a day or two."

"What are you going to say to Chuza?" Mary asked.

"Nothing," Joanna said defensively, knowing all along how ridiculous it sounded.

"Herod's troops will never find the bandits even if they try. They might be half way to Egypt by now."

"True, and I hope we never see them again."

- - -

Two days later, Joanna was still in Magdala, but knew she had to head home and face Chuza. However, the fear instilled by the robbers nearly stifled any thought of travel. She didn't feel like making the trip back home by herself, knowing the robbers might still be out there somewhere.

Mary noticed the concern on Joanna's face, and promptly packed a few things herself.

"You're coming too?" Joanna said, hopefully.

"Yes, you don't want to travel alone, do you?"

Joanna shook her head.

Mary took her by the arm, and together they limped out the gate and down the road toward Tiberias. Joanna breathed in the fresh air. It was a beautiful day, filled with the songs of larks and sparrows as they flitted in and out of bushes alongside the path. Here and there, the odd bird sat alone out on the prairie grass. The wind moved the grass in gentle waves, and the warmth of its breeze was welcomed by Mary and Joanna as they walked.

A beautiful day—not much different from the day we were terrorized! Joanna briefly thought. What little conversation they had, dropped off as they passed by the very place of their previous misfortune. They quickened their pace. Joanna felt her muscles tightening as she advanced along the trail. Both of them glanced over their shoulders, across the hillsides, and especially ahead on the path. Only after they completely passed by the ambush spot, did they speak.

Joanna was first. "At least I can walk without a limp now."

Mary hadn't realized her breathing had been short and shallow, but now she let out a sigh and said, "Yes.... much better." She turned from staring down the path to look at Joanna. "So what are you going to tell Chuza?"

"Don't know... Maybe he won't come home until after dark. I'll leave the lamp down low."

"You know he'll see it!" Mary assessed, "I think he'll be very upset!"

"Perhaps he'll forbid me to come and visit you."

"There's a chance. So what will you do?" Mary peered at her.

"I'll think of something. I can't stand to stay in Tiberias all the time. There's no fun! The palace is a continual charade of dignitaries, pretending to be interested in things that don't matter."

They both chuckled dryly at the obvious truth.

They arrived at Tiberias, and headed straight towards Joanna's house on the other side of the palace. Joanna threw a veil over her face to accomplish her purpose, but at the moment they passed the palace, they met Chuza hurrying out the gate. He instantly spotted Joanna, and strode over to her.

At first he didn't notice her injuries. "Joanna, I need you to attend to the accounting roo...m." No sooner had he asked when he saw her eye, a dark spot that was easily visible, even through the veil. He moved closer and lifted her veil.

"What in Caesar's name happened?" he demanded.

She re-lived the trauma. The picture appeared in her mind; the face of a man, taunting her... His ugly head was turned sideways, and through his disgustingly broken yellowed teeth, he growled, "...the next time, we will kill you!"

Joanna felt her throat tighten again, and her chest began to heave. She tried to put a hand on Chuza's shoulder for support. Finally, she couldn't hold back the tears. "We were robbed on the way to Magdala!" she sobbed. She glanced up at Chuza for a moment, with her head still bowed. He continued to prod his fingers around the bruised area of her eye, like a physician diagnosing the extent of the wound.

Joanna wished he would simply hold her! She wished he would just forget the stupid bruise! She even leaned forward slightly. Put your arms around me and comfort me!

Instead, Chuza pushed her to an upright position, and blurted, "Well, you can't be seen at the palace like that. Who knows what people will think! No, you better go home and do something to get your eye healed up."

Mary had been standing nearby. She dared not intervene, but couldn't believe his lack of compassion.

Now Chuza marched off the same direction he first had intended to go, leaving Joanna standing with Mary.

"Alright, if it has to be that way..." Joanna sniffled, "then I'll fix it myself. I always do!"

She wiped the tears off her cheeks with the back of her hand, grabbed Mary's arm, and they made their way to her home. She could only hope that time would help Chuza to change his cold matter-of-fact demeanor.

Whether or not Chuza had found a change in compassion, the very next day, Chuza rushed through the door with the grand announcement: They would be going on a trip; this time, with Herod.

Chapter Eleven

Caesar Versus Religion

A trip to Rome! Joanna could hardly contain her excitement. The ship rounded the south boot of Italy, and headed northward up the coast.

"We're almost there!" she exclaimed. She leaned over the oak railing of the sturdy sea vessel to see the spray from the ship's hull. Chuza had been by her side for days, and it had been wonderful! The first three days of traveling overland had been a little tough, but now far behind her. For the last seventeen, they had traveled by ship, and how she loved the Mediterranean Sea! Chuza reached over and held her arm.

"Don't get too excited Joanna. We don't want to be picking you out of the waters!"

She straightened up and smiled; first at him, then at the picturesque scene. Chuza, the gentle flapping of the sails, the sea birds, the cerulean blue of the sky... Ahh! Yes! The dream of a lifetime. She enjoyed every moment with her husband, not being tempted by any illicit encounters such as in Galilee. Herod had even been civil the entire trip, and she felt honored to accompany the king. She would be there when the ship docked and the report given to Tiberias Caesar Augustus. What an incredible trip!

Now she saw the Port of Ostia appearing in the distant mist. The ships anchored in the port grew more distinct as their ship edged closer. Now she could already see the flags they flew, of Spain and of France. Other ornate ships flew unrecognizable flags from distant lands. Dozens of such vessels dotted the bay. They had come to do trade with Rome. Along the port, many buildings of various sorts studded the sky. Just off from the port, the clear waters of the Mediterranean changed to an emerald green where the Tiber River shed its waters into the sea. Beautiful boulders protruded from the shoreline throughout the bay. Joanna lifted her head, and smelled the salty, but clean fragrance of the Mediterranean. A short time after, she could see the slaves running up and down the ramps, unloading goods destined for Rome.

Soon Joanna's ship would be at Ostia, and the trading ships would have to make way for their vessel, since it belonged to the mighty Roman Empire.

The sailors aboard Joanna's ship began to drop and gather several sails as they approached the port. When they arrived in Ostia, children greeted them by waiving Roman flags on the dock. People by the hundreds stood, cheering, as the ship slowly inched its way closer. Caesar came down to the dock and personally welcomed Herod and his staff. Special attendants looked after their luggage, and sergeants walked with them from the ship to land. A convoy of soldiers on horses, dressed in Roman attire waited for them on land. Caesar stopped and waved to crowd. But his eyes were glued on the ship. He didn't move until they finished unloading the most important cargo.

A centurion, with his one hundred men, rushed up the planks onto the ship, and quickly secured the leather bags—all of which contained the Galilean taxation collection. They turned and proceeded to pile them high on ox-carts destined for Rome. The port of Ostia was only one hundred thirty furlongs from the massive city of a million people. Special guards of Rome brought over an enclosed carriage pulled by two stallions, for Caesar, Herod, and Joanna to travel in. The entire procession began to move along a wide, paved road toward Rome. Caesar glanced over his shoulder and smiled approvingly at the sight of the incoming wealth.

The road made its way along the beautiful Tiber River. Its luscious green waters tumbled over rocks. Along its shores many trees stood twenty to thirty cubits high. Fishermen took full advantage of the trees. Many of them had boats tied to various trees, and they worked in the shade, cleaning their nets.

Soon the river gave way to the buildings at the edge of the city.

Rome, the 'Eternal City!' This is going to be wonderful, she thought to herself. This might be as good as eternal bliss!

She imagined the sights and scenes around the markets. She would chat with people of other cultures—just to find out how they lived in distant places. Sailors from all over the world would be in Rome. She imagined herself asking people about Spain, Persia, India, and beyond—places filled with stories of treasure and adventure. In a way, she would be part of their adventures just by listening to their stories. Just walking the streets of Rome would be a glorious adventure in itself.

The three-some joined a large entourage in the center of Rome, and walked toward the palace. Thousands lined the streets, following their king with his guests. The sound of cheering was deafening. At the palace, Caesar dismissed the attending servants, and waved good-bye to everyone in the parade. Then he welcomed Herod, Chuza and Joanna into the inner court, past two more guards, and finally into his throne room.

Herod was allowed to approach Caesar's throne, but in accordance with protocol, Chuza and Joanna remained well off to the side. Joanna was riveted by the magnificent structure. Several columns decorated the throne room. The top of each column was designed with flowered leaves growing upward. Each corner at the top had four circular "ears". The main vertical of each column consisted of elegant fluting from ground to top.

Caesar proceeded to commend Herod for his "discreetness, fairness, and shrewdness in collecting taxation."

He smiled coyly at the corners of his mouth as he spoke, "I heard you expanded your realm of taxation into the hill country of Galilee and Capernaum. Good work, Herod!

"It may be possible that some of our subjects have been taxed by you and taxed again by your brother Philip. But do not worry my friend. Be assured this is no real problem. To be a subject in the great kingdom of Rome has too many benefits for them to complain of over-taxation. They will survive, and of course we survive, yes?"

Later, as Herod, Chuza, and Joanna walked briskly toward their sleeping quarters, they passed by a group of twenty to thirty Roman soldiers. Their bright red uniforms glistened in the setting sun. Helmets had been polished to a perfect shine. Their swords reflected the powerful rays of sun's light. They stood in a line, motionless, staring straight ahead. However, what went unnoticed by Herod was certainly noticed by Joanna.

She took a sharp breath. The third soldier from the end was someone she had seen before. No! It cannot be, she thought to herself. But there was no mistake. The man held the distinct smooth skin of people from the east. His bony nose was long and straight. Thick eyebrows protruded in a straight line. A wicked smile extending from ear to ear revealed one broken tooth among the other yellow ones. Yes—this was the same person. He was one of the bandits who had attacked Mary and her on the road to Magdala. He was the very one who had put his boot on her neck, grinding her face in the ground, and making her fear for her life.

Joanna turned her head the other way and veiled her face. Had he recognized her? What was he doing in Rome, in a Roman uniform? She had believed the bandits were simple thieves, more interested in robbery than anything. But this changed the whole picture. The man was sinister, evil, and deceptive. How did he become a Roman soldier so quickly?

Chuza and Joanna were almost past the group, when the soldier's captain let out a sharp command, followed by a lower "take ease." The soldiers left their rigid alignment, and grouped in a relaxed semi-circle.

Joanna took a quick look over her shoulder. Had he seen her? It didn't appear so, because he began to chat casually with the other soldiers. Joanna consoled herself with a final quick glance through her veil, and observed the man continuing to converse with the others. He hadn't recognized her. She sighed in relief, but still had a lot of questions.

Joanna wondered how she should react to what she had just witnessed. Should she tell Chuza? She wished more than anything that Mary was with her. But she was not.

Joanna thought about the robbery on the roadside, and realized Mary and her could have just as easily been killed. Now she remembered what Chuza had told her about Parthian soldiers: They had to commit either a robbery or a sword fight to the death before they qualified to be a soldier. She and Mary had been robbed. It might be possible they were Parthian! And now one of them had infiltrated the Roman army! She looked away.

She also thought of Namen and Ephraim, and his amorous advances on the way to Tiberias. She hadn't told Chuza about them, and there was no doubt about their nationality!

Joanna's imagination played tricks on her. She imagined this wicked man might know where they stayed. She felt the tightness in her throat again, brought on by fear. He might even know that Chuza would be attending several meetings at the palace and Joanna would be left alone. Would this soldier seek her out and harm her? Oh, if there ever was a time when she needed protection, it was now. She could feel the insecurity of being a foreigner in a strange city. In her isolation, she felt a deep longing, almost an audible groaning within, for something or someone to help—someone who would care. She needed someone who would bring security even if it meant standing up to her sins. Most of all, she wished for someone to forgive her past.

At this time, above any time in her life, she needed protection of heart. She needed the comfort and affection of someone strong, who would put his arms around her and truly love her. She needed a stabilizing factor—a person who would really care about her well-being. Someone who would not leave her in a time of trial.

That night, Joanna woke up with a start. During the deep of night, a strange sound clattered in the adjacent kitchen. She froze! Someone had crept into their room! Her heart pounded wildly. Her breath seemed unbearably loud as hot dry air released from her lungs. Her throat felt dry and hard.

She reached over to touch her husband, and to her dismay, Chuza was gone.

"Chuza?" she ventured in fear, hoping he had caused the noise. There was no answer.

"Chuza, is that you?" She spoke a bit louder, but her words seemed muffled by the stone walls. Again, no answer came. Now her heart began to pound in fear.

Suddenly, the door to the lavatory opened and a light shone out.

"You don't have to get so panicky, Joanna! I was just relieving myself."

Joanna breathed a sigh of relief, but her heart still pounded. Why did fear grip her so? Perhaps all the nights of being with other men now haunted her. Maybe those engagements had left some sort of mistrust deep in her conscience. Would she have to live the rest of her life in fear and torment because of her sin? She pushed the thought to the furthest corner of her mind, but she still shook.

Chuza came to the bedside, and, pulling back the soft covering of sheepskin, slid under them. He snuggled close to Joanna, and she felt his arm around her shoulders and his hand pushing gently against the midpoint of her back.

She melted in his arms! This was the security she longed for. This was the protection she had always desired! She nestled close, putting her arms warmly under his arms and around his back. They locked in a tight embrace. Nothing else mattered now. No tainted past, no fear could harm her now. The moment bore no pretense. She tightened her grip on her husband, and he didn't seem to mind a bit. She had married Chuza for such moments, and he was the very reason for living. He was her refuge, and the source of the most wonderful feelings of safety, love, and ecstasy in the world! Chuza would protect her. His love for her was constant and she could depend on his faithfulness.

Morning came, and the sun shone through the window from a brilliant Roman sky. The warm solar rays brought hope of a prosperous day. She had made plans to visit the riverside shops and many other fabulous places. She planned to tour all of Rome in one day if she could.

However, having time to herself offered a mixed blessing. Rome provided fun and adventure and she loved to explore this wonder of the world. But at the same time, with so much time to herself, she found herself drawn back into the temptations to indulge in less than pure pleasures.

In fact, the first place she visited was such a trap. She walked from market to market along the Tiber. Several soldiers gathered in groups in parks and city squares. Compared to Galilee, Rome bustled with activity. People clambered to get to their destinations. Carts clattered along the stone streets everywhere. The humidity and heat kept anyone from being comfortable, but didn't stop them from socializing.

Joanna soon found herself flirting with a number of the soldiers. Before long, she attracted a mob of men, all laughing hysterically at silly jokes, and their eyes riveted on her beauty. She felt herself impulsively drawn to some of the most handsome of them.

She loved it, and she hated it. Why did she always have to be tortured? What was this impelling force that so drew her to sin. It defied any human reasoning. Why would she want to hurt Chuza so? She was far too willing to compromise the vows she had made with him. She didn't understand her feelings. She tried to put the conflict out of her mind, but it would not go. Again, and again, like a wave, the thoughts came upon her and thrust her into a life of imagination, indulgence and sinful pleasure.

This time, however, she did not follow through with her urging. For one, she was alone in a far-away city. Secondly, her wandering thoughts were now awakened by the sound of horsemen galloping towards her. The Roman soldiers! She flung her veil over her face, and stooping down, rushed into the nearest shop.

After she was sure they had left, she walked across the street to a public garden. She found a bench near a shady tree, and sat down, weeping. Oh, why do I have to feel this way? Why am I so afraid all the time? What is going to happen to me?

That afternoon, in response to Caesar's invitation, Joanna and Chuza attended the Arena-stadio in Rome. She had been promised a dramatic show. They were going to watch lions killing prisoners, and executions in such manner never seen by them. Joanna wasn't so impressed, though. She didn't consider blood and guts to be entertainment at all.

Chuza marched alongside of Herod while Joanna tried to keep up.

"I've never seen the gladiators before," Chuza mused, "Kind of ugly in a way, isn't it?"

"Don't forget, these are men convicted to die, Chuza," Herod remarked, "Some of them are murderers and all of them are enemies to the Roman government"

"Still, it seems like a cruel way for someone to die."

Joanna swallowed at the thought of seeing the torture of prisoners. 'Execution by the lion's jaw,' Herod had described it.

They arrived at the Arena-stadio about mid-day, just in time to squeeze through the narrow corridors which led into the seating area. Trained slave-masters brought out the first of many prisoners. They unshackled him, and pushed him onto the field, in full view of everyone. A loud roar came from across the field and echoed around the stands. Joanna looked to see why the people cheered. Across the flat field a door opened slowly and from inside that door, a lion appeared. He was a majestic beast. In one sense, he looked as friendly as Herod's pet cats. Padding out into the center of the field, the lion seemed baffled by the noise of the thousands in attendance. He sniffed the air. Then, his eyes focused in on the slave — a lone figure across the field. He began moving towards the prisoner. Suddenly the lion sprinted toward him. The slave screamed and tried to climb the wall, but slipped down as people poked at him from above. Frantically, he ran along the base of the wall, but the lion leaped upon him in a split second, and with one bite to the neck, brought instant death.

The crowd chanted, "Long live King Caesar! Long live King Caesar!"

Joanna tried to focus on other things; the seats, the people in the crowd, the clothing she wore. They had been given the best seats in the amphitheatre. Theirs had an awning above, in case of rain. The luxury was not afforded to most people, but provided only for Caesar's guests of honor. She adored the suite far more than the event. Several sentries guarded their seats, and she was even within speaking distance with King Caesar.

"Do you like the 'Arena-stadio?'" Caesar asked looking at Chuza and Joanna.

"Very much," replied Chuza, "I can see that it is nearly full today."

"Yes, and I have plans to begin construction on a larger one. It may take a number of years to build, but it will exceed any sporting house in the world. I will call it 'The Coliseum.'"

"That will be an impressive place. Perhaps I will get to see it someday."

"Herod tells me that you are doing a tremendous job as his steward. If that continues, you might indeed return to Rome after the Coliseum is built.

"On the other hand, the Coliseum will be so grand, that it may take a long time to build, even beyond my lifetime."

More lions appeared from the same metal den. The slave-masters whipped their prisoners onto the field with the lions. After several of them had been offered to the lions, they began to move whole parties of prisoners into the field. Sometimes the groups would huddle together in fear, hoping to protect one another. But the lions would dive into the center of the groups grasping one by the leg, another by the ankle, and shake them with their massive head until they were rendered unconscious. Screams upon screams rang out in the arena. Eventually, the lions satisfied their appetites, and moved back, one by one, into their dens at the far side of the field. When the last one reached the den, the gate began to move once again, and clanged shut.

Immediately a number of arena servants ran out on to the field and removed what was left of the bodies of those mauled by the lions. Others set up torches on several poles.

"What is that for?" Joanna asked Chuza. "Who are those people?"

Soldiers marched about a dozen men and women wearing simple prisoner clothing toward the poles. They chained them, hand and feet, to the poles while the torches blazed above them.

"Now we will see the elimination of the real enemies to Rome," Herod declared to Chuza.

Caesar leaned over to Herod and asked, "Do you suppose, Herod, there are people in Galilee who are enemies of Rome?"

Herod understood well where Caesar was going with the question. If he bared the details of every problem in Galilee, Caesar would say he had not kept order. If he said there were no enemies of Rome in Galilee, surely Caesar would recognize his evading reply.

Herod compromised, "From time to time we do have uprisings, but you can be sure our soldiers are quick to put down anything that would be a threat. In fact, I recently had to execute a steward called Stephanus, who was stealing money."

"Indeed, I did hear that report. Good work, Herod!

"Understand this: Anyone who is against Rome, whether politically, economically, or even religiously must be quickly disposed of." Caesar smiled and glanced over at Herod to make sure he had heard.

Herod bobbed his head up and down as Caesar spoke.

"Yes, sometimes the religious ones are the worst. Do you have any religious uprisings in Galilee?"

Herod responded, "There is a man called John the Baptist, but he simply amuses me. He's no threat to Galilee or Rome. Oh, yes... there is one other... this Jesus fellow, but I don't know much about Him."

Caesar was quick to interrupt Herod, "You be careful with those religious leaders and their followers. There is only one god in the Roman Empire, and I am he."

"Yes, of course," Herod replied.

Soon the event at the arena ended, and they stood to leave.

Caesar said, "Herod, I would like you to come with me. We have a number of matters to discuss before the evening. Chuza, I would like for you to go with my guard to meet two of my stewards who assist me here in Rome. They will be of ultimate value to your work as steward for Herod. Joanna, you will be escorted to your accommodations."

A guard promptly came over and directed Joanna to follow him down the well-worn path away from the Arena-stadio.

"Could we stop at a couple of shops on the way?" Joanna asked.

The guard agreed without hesitation. "It will be my honor to do so."

"I have another request," she ventured, "Do you think you could find someone to do a special favor for me?"

"I have been instructed to help you with whatever you ask," the guard said.

- - -

About two hours later, Chuza appeared at the door of her accommodations. He had no idea what was about to transpire.

"Surprise!" Joanna sung.

The room was filled with the aroma of cooking food. Five minstrels began playing their flutes and lyres in the corner. The chef procured by Joanna's guard stood over a rich roasted meal of fatted calf, sided with local vegetables, fruit samples, and lentils imported from Egypt. Fresh bread made from wheat, beans and millet was artfully centered in the middle of the table.

"What's this?" Chuza exclaimed, his jaw dropping, looking at the food, then the musicians, then Joanna.

"Aren't you hungry? This is for my incredible, wonderful husband!" Joanna slid over to Chuza, and happily embraced him with both arms.

"This will certainly be a night to remember!" he smiled back and forth at each of the people in the room. "Thank you! You're incredible, Joanna!" With that he returned the embrace, and kissed her affectionately.

Joanna leaned her head against his shoulder, and smiled broadly as their eyes met.

Chapter Twelve

Joanna's Choice

Just a few days after returning from Rome, Joanna stared across the open fields from her vantage point on the palace wall behind her home. The knolls of grass waved with each fresh breeze that flowed from the hilltops and down across the slopes. Soon her thoughts drifted to her present situation in Tiberias. Since returning from Rome, nothing had really changed; Chuza was still over-worked, Herod had reverted to his ugly self, Crabolus still flitted about trying to impress everybody, and Mary still pursued her men.

She chuckled as she thought how different Mary and she were. They were from two very different economic levels. She supported Chuza's work at the royal palace, but Mary wasn't tied to any steady employment. She was a city lady, but Mary was a small town woman. She was married, but Mary was single. Of course that didn't make for a great difference since both of them went for the party's impetuous characters.

Joanna stared ahead, oblivious to the summer clouds as they slowly moved across the sky. She felt a slight tinge of guilt, and deducted that her aberrant actions contributed to the coldness between her and Chuza. However, she could always come up with a reason to shift blame to Chuza or Herod for the impasse.

This had been the case when, upon returning from Rome, she had immediately left the house to catch up on the latest news at friends' homes.

Later, when she met Chuza at work, he asked her, "Where were you?"

Joanna immediately became defensive, retorting sarcastically, "I was traveling back from Rome with you, wasn't I?"

Chuza had muttered something incomprehensible to Joanna, and that had ended the conversation.

It seemed her expression of good will to Chuza had evaporated into contention once again. He was busy, and she was disappointed, so she headed home.

Now the sun slowly slipped over the horizon. Joanna moved inside to avoid the cold breeze that slid down the mountain slopes at this time every night.

Joanna had lit several lamps by the time Chuza arrived home. She heard his footsteps nearing their home, and stood up to greet him. It was all Joanna could do to hide her disappointment. She swallowed twice, and tried hard to put on a good front. "Hi soldier! How was your day?"

"Long and hard. Herod desperately needs to pick some attendants who can think straight."

"Well, since you worked long and hard, you must have gotten lots done then," she said, trying to keep the conversation positive.

Chuza didn't offer an immediate reply, which left Joanna trying to figure out a way to tell him about her plans. She just had to go to Magdala!

There were two reasons to go to Magdala, she decided. One, to get together with her best friend Mary, and the other, to go to a party. Inevitably the party would lead to dancing and drunkenness and possibly to an overnight tussle with one of the young men. She needed to be there to protect Mary, she reasoned shallowly. Mary belonged to the wilder side and Joanna recalled saving her from getting hurt more than once.

But the paradox of the matter was this: She, of her own volition, vacillated between being Mary's 'helper', and actually desiring the forbidden fruit herself.

"I've been wondering how Mary is doing," she started to relay to Chuza, "I think I should go and see her."

"Maybe next week. Right now is not good. Things are busy," Chuza said as though it were decided so simply.

"Perhaps things are busy for you Chuza, but I'm getting bored out of my mind."

"Well, you can't take off every time you get bored. I can't take the time to cook and clean when I don't get home till night."

"I'm not going because I'm bored," Joanna stuttered, "Mary needs me. She has no husband—no one to look after her at all."

"We just got back from Rome, and I don't want you taking off on—who knows what you're doing! And don't forget what happened the last time you traveled to Magdala. You got robbed, and beaten up quite badly as I remember it." Chuza turned and stared at her for a moment. "I told you then to not be wandering off to Magdala anymore. It's just too dangerous. You can help me sort things out at the accounting office. That way you'll not be bored."

"But I haven't seen Mary since we left for Rome!"

Chuza snorted, and muttered as he walked to the next room, "Work to be done here. And lot's of it!" Silence ensued.

Joanna knew he was angry. When Chuza became upset, he withdrew. She couldn't argue with someone who didn't speak. She deducted there were two choices: One, she could cancel her plans and please Chuza or, two; she could leave for Magdala in the morning and suffer the consequences of Chuza's cold shoulder for weeks.

All night long she tossed and turned in frustration. How could Chuza treat me like that? Just because he was stupidly busy, didn't mean she needed to be. After all, what cleaning needed to be done when they hadn't even been at home to mess anything up? No, Chuza was being totally unreasonable to demand she stay home.

At daybreak, Chuza jumped out of bed, and moments later, left for the palace. Joanna cried a silent cry of exhaustion. Her throat was parched and her eyes were dry. Deep within, she understood the struggle. Despite her defensive arguments, the real struggle existed between doing the honorable thing and doing the exciting thing.

For an hour she walked back and forth. She stopped and stared at her wardrobe. She walked over to the window, and looked blankly out towards the east and north.

I hate him!

Mechanically, she packed a change of clothes and answered her inner beckoning while blocking out the thoughts of reason and commitment to Chuza. The gate squealed shut behind her.

Joanna had made her choice. She didn't want to dwell on the reasons, but she continued to fume over Chuza's selfishness. She kicked the odd stone along the path with her shoe, hard enough to hurt. Chuza could work himself to the bone for Herod if he wanted, but she wasn't going to let it affect her.

With relief, she took the final steps along the street, and up the path to Mary's door. She had already laid out the plans in her mind. This afternoon she would tell Mary all about her trip to Rome, and tonight they would party. She got to the front door, which, to her surprise swung open. Mary had seen her coming. Mary welcomed her in with a quick gesture and a hearty hug.

Joanna immediately spotted the other two men in the room, Ephraim, and Namen. Obviously Mary had been up to something again.

"I believe you already know both Ephraim and Namen."

Joanna did a half bow before the men and then quickly turned to Mary with a questioning look on her face.

Mary released her hug, and grasped the white perfume box, holding it up to show Joanna.

"Do you remember the gift box I received? Namen is my secret admirer!"

"Oh, yes. Of course!" Joanna hardly remembered meeting him at the party, but instantly recalled the aroma of the gift left at Mary's door. "So you are the one!" she said, and almost spoke out loud ...ah, yes, the amorous Namen!

She looked him over. He was very handsome, with edged eyebrows, trimmed black hair and a chiseled chin, making him look quite intelligent. She also remembered that he was a Parthian, and if anything like Ephraim, he would also be quite biased in his opinions of Roman rule. As it turned out, Namen was even twice as much the critic.

"Mary tells me you have lived in Tiberias for seven years," Namen started.

"Um hmm," Joanna said uninterestedly.

"Doesn't it bother you when Herod is taxing the Galilean people to death?"

"Is that what you think?" The moment Joanna said it, she wished she hadn't. Why open up a conversation with someone so steeped in believing their own version of right and wrong.

"It's not only what I think. The whole region of Galilee agrees. ...as does your friend here."

Joanna was astounded at their directness. They didn't let up a bit either. Over the next twenty minutes or so, they continued to try to persuade Mary and her of the Parthian advantage. They even suggested the "Roman oppression" would soon be over. From time to time, they threw in a question to Joanna, or a point to prove they were right.

"There is a man right here in Magdala," they stated, "who was taxed by Philip, and then the tax collector from Herod came and made him pay taxes again, and double the amount at that." He gestured his hand outward toward Joanna to emphasize the point. "I can take you to him if you don't believe me."

"OK, I believe you," Joanna gave in. There was no point in arguing, and besides, she knew double taxing was a regular practice of both Herod of Galilee, and his brother Philip the tetrarch of the northern regions of Iturea and Traconitus.

Soon the conversation switched to the party to take place that night. Joanna suspected the party was really being put on by Namen, Ephraim, and their friends. But tolerating them might be worth a fun night out. After all, she convinced herself, men were men, and it shouldn't matter much whether they were Jewish, Roman, or Parthian.

That being decided upon, she dismissed her serious, questioning voice, and spoke with her giddy, party voice. "I think I live for parties," she stated, with a slight wink.

"The party tonight is being arranged by the two of us," Namen informed her, confirming her suspicions. He motioned his hand to Ephraim and back, "and we are so glad you are coming. I guarantee you will have a good time."

Joanna turned to them and smiled, "I like to party," she said, emphasizing the word "like" in a rising tone. "So where is this party going to be?" she smiled as she asked.

The two men returned a smile, noting the progress they were making, "It's just down the road at the large house on the corner."

As they continued describing the details of the party, she soon discovered some serious implications if she chose to attend. Now that Joanna had agreed to attend the party, they began their real quest for Joanna.

"Since we are putting on a party for you tonight, we would also like you to do a favor for us."

"Favor?" She chuckled. Joanna figured she knew what that meant! What a bold way to ask for an overnight affair. Most men she had encountered were more subtle in their approach. She thought perhaps Parthian culture was more insensitive than that of the Romans.

"Yes a favor," they replied, "Tomorrow, we would like you to meet us at the Magdala Inn. We have a proposal which will make you very rich."

Joanna took a breath to try to hide her surprise. "How rich? And what is the proposal you speak of?"

"We will lay out the proposal to you tomorrow. But know this: Just by showing up, we will pay you forty denarii. And if you should decide to help us, we could possibly pay you a hundred times that."

Joanna calculated the amount easily. Forty times a hundred made four thousand. Four thousand denarii would buy her a lot of fashionable clothes. She liked the idea, but didn't like the idea of helping the Parthians. Neither was forty denarii or even a multiple thereof her idea of "rich."

"You want me to do something against Rome?"

"We want you to help your friend Mary, here, and others like her living in Magdala."

"I don't know..." said Joanna.

Mary strode over to Namen, put her arm around him, and peered over his shoulder at Joanna. "You see, Joanna, these boys are really quite sweet!"

Joanna tried not to show how perplexed she was. Something had changed with Mary. Joanna had often observed Mary as a flirt, but Mary's obsession with Namen couldn't be supported. Mary stroked the back of her hand across Namen's neck, and at the same time, lifted her leg up and around Namen's waist. "See, Joanna," her voice lowered until it sounded like another's, "He's got me!" The whispered, raspy way in which she spoke, actually scared Joanna. She almost left the room. Mary was behaving beyond anything reasonable. Some evil force seemed to be controlling her.

"Mary!" Joanna whispered, pulling her off to the side, "Are you sure you want to do this?"

"Of course! What's the problem?"

"No problem I guess..." Joanna said, still in shock. But the problem had been real. Mary behaved crudely and spoke in a more perverse manner than ever.

Joanna also faced another problem, her own problem. She tried to deal with the same compelling force she always wrestled with. Boredom, frustration, and discontent all produced a squeeze effect on her heart. For years now, she had readily submitted to the quest for adventure, and obeyed the inner yearnings. Now she began to fear where it all might end up.

Joanna shook herself, and tried to respond to the two men. "Well. Anyway, tonight we party. Tomorrow can wait."

By evening, Joanna felt better about going to the party. She put on the evening gown she had brought with her for the occasion. She had purchased it while in Rome, and brought it with her for a purpose just like this. And the men noticed too. In their usual Parthian boldness, they heaped accolades of commendation on Joanna, to the point of making her blush. And when she blushed, the men smiled.

The men led the way towards the door, and Mary jumped up to follow. Joanna shrugged her shoulders, and stood as well, "I guess tonight we party!" Forget the expectations of everybody else! she reasoned. I'm going to have a good time! Forget Herod. Forget Tiberias. Forget Chuza. He would have to cope with all the problems back home, and he shouldn't expect me to be part of them.

She entered the darkened doorway of the corner building, and was greeted by the sound of flutes, stringed dulcimers, and horns. Joanna was surprised at how many of the common people attended. It was evident they all enjoyed the presence, and funding, of the Parthian sponsors.

Joanna loved the unrestricted atmosphere in the room. While Roman parties had to be strictly monitored and regulated by Herod's soldiers, this was truly a party of the people. The sponsors of the party, namely Ephraim and Namen, actively took part in dancing, and flirting with all the women of the town. That being said, few people indulged in more liquor than they could handle. As a result, far less impropriety occurred than at a Roman feast. Joanna liked it.

She dove in the festivities with a broad smile and a light foot. Dancing, twirling, skittering from one side to another, she laughed and giggled, especially when she happened to run into another person.

She also noted that the Parthian men were very expressive in the use of their fingers and hands by creating quick waves in the air, and allowing their hands to lead their bodies. It was certainly a dance with a Persian flavor. Many of the local women loved it too, and had followed the men's example by using their hands and fingers in like manner.

"Isn't this great!" Mary exclaimed as she passed Joanna on the floor in opposite directions.

"Wonderful! Delicious!" Joanna called back as she disappeared behind other dancers.

The music continued far into the night. Finally, the musicians put down their instruments out of exhaustion, and all the happy and contented hearts of Magdala began to leave for home.

"Those Parthians sure know how to treat us Galileans!" Mary stated enthusiastically as she and Joanna walked up the street toward her home.

"I had fun," Joanna agreed. However, for the first time that night, she thought about Chuza. He would have no doubt discovered her absent many hours ago. But it was highly unlikely he would come after her. He would easily guess where she went, and though he didn't like it, he wouldn't think it worth the risk of traveling by night to retrieve her. Neither would he think it worth the confrontation, and the bother of arguing all the way back to Tiberias. So, figuring she knew what Chuza would be thinking, Joanna simply walked in with Mary, and called it a night.

Tomorrow would be another day, and another choice to make. Would she give allegiance to Parthia or Rome? Joanna shrugged her shoulders and lay down on her bed to sleep.

Chapter Thirteen

The Parthian Proposal

After breakfast the next morning, Joanna walked briskly down from Mary's home to the glistening white stone structure. The air was already filled with the sound of braying donkeys and camels, calling for their owners to bring them their early morning feed.

The Inn of Magdala was a small structure compared to those in Jerusalem, but all Magdalenes were surprised how often its rooms filled to capacity. Many stopped by the inn to enjoy the nearby Sea of Galilee and rest by its serene shores. Others traveled on their way to Jerusalem for business. Some came to fish, and some came because they were people of influence; soldiers, tax collectors, messengers, and political leaders. Not that Parthians were considered political leaders, but as far as the innkeeper was concerned, a shekel was a shekel, and Parthian travelers were as welcome as any other nationality.

Joanna however, wasn't interested in the business of inn keeping. She was trying to decide whether to support the Parthians or not. The environment of espionage could not be dismissed. Meddling undercover was dangerous, and it made her quite uncomfortable. Nevertheless, she had promised to show up, and so she nervously approached the inn.

Joanna entered the inn, and rapped on the third door from the end. She waited for a response from the Parthians, shuffling her feet back and forth on the cobbled stone. Within moments, the door swung open, and Ephraim and Namen beckoned Joanna to come in, and closed the door behind her. She entered their room, noting the occupants had been given one of the best rooms at the inn. The room overlooked the sea, which shimmered in the early morning sun. They motioned for Joanna to take a seat.

"We have looked forward to this moment for a long time," Ephraim began, "and this is the beginning of freedom for Judea."

Oh, the 'freedom' word again! Joanna thought to herself.

"We were very grateful when the innkeeper offered us this room." He swept his hand across the room, showing the highlighted marble trim, and beautiful wooden furniture. "The people of Judea are so supportive of our cause," he continued with an edged smile at the corners of his mouth. This beautiful room and the wonderful sea here — so much better than our usual barracks!"

"You stay in barracks near here?" Joanna asked.

Namen took over for Ephraim at this point, and leaned forward on his chair. He looked out from under his projecting black eyebrows straight toward Joanna. "We are posted at our barracks just north of Caesarea Philippi. We eat and sleep in tents. Yes, this is an unusual and welcomed treat—thanks to the generous people of Magdala."

"You have a beautiful view of the Sea of Tiberias," Joanna ventured.

"We prefer to call it the Sea of Galilee," Namen stated, "The Sea of 'Tiberias' is only what Herod named it."

John 6:1 "... the Sea of Galilee, which is the Sea of Tiberias."

Ephraim glanced over at Joanna several times, but she stared at an invisible object on the floor. He smiled again, just enough to show a line of white teeth between his lips.

"Our purpose today is to request your help. Since you are friendly to the cause, and because you are Mary's friend, we trust you, and believe you will want to help us. What we need is information."

Joanna remembered information equaled reward, and the promised reward was indeed a generous payment.

"I'll tell you what I can about Tiberias, or the palace," she offered meekly.

"Our plan is to change the oppression Herod places over the land. People hate the man. Once Herod is dealt with, we can then address the need to remove the tax collectors."

"And what do you intend to do with Herod?" Joanna stuttered.

Ephraim continued, "We are at this moment watching his every move, and the movement of all his men: the soldiers, the guards, the servants, and of course the stewards. Make no mistake; we are discovering every area of Herod's weakness! You know of Herod's many weaknesses, don't you?" He laughed in ridicule as he belittled Herod.

Joanna was taken aback by the mention of them watching the stewards. If they watched the stewards, then surely they watched the chief steward! Her devotion to Chuza was the one thing preventing her from giving complete allegiance to the Parthians as Mary had done. But money was money, and she looked forward to her 'reward'.

After laughing about Herod's weaknesses, the man promptly swore, and then expanded on his revelation of the tax collectors. "Those publicans... Why, they are Jews themselves, working for Herod the Roman. So they turn against their friends to bow to Rome! Can you imagine stealing from your own countrymen? Is it any wonder they are despised by all the civilians of Galilee?"

The Parthian continued, "We do not bow to Herod or Caesar, or their money grabbing associates. The people of Galilee don't honor Herod either. On the other hand, you *do* understand that all the people show utmost respect for us, yes?" Ephraim stared at Joanna noting her questioning eyebrows.

Joanna nodded. "Yes, I understand how people feel about taxes." Understand she did, but the way Ephraim had tilted the facts made her cringe within. Herod might be in the category of the despised, but to think of Chuza described as a "money grabbing associate" was another matter.

"Your husband is a steward of Herod, correct?" Ephraim queried.

"Yes. He doesn't know that I..."

Namen interrupted her, "Yes, but we understand your husband is not always satisfied to work with Herod."

"Who told you that?" Joanna said, taking care to not look them straight in the eye.

Ignoring the question, Namen continued, "We need you to tell us where the keys to Herod's quarters are kept. We cannot complete the mission without installing a Parthian king for Galilee. The people must all know who is in command."

Ephraim now asked a direct question: "Does your husband keep the keys in his accounting room, or do the guards or soldiers keep some of the keys?"

Joanna pondered what she was about to reveal. To tell them the location of the keys would put Chuza squarely in the face of danger. She took another look at the men's shining swords hanging loosely by their sides, and said, "Chuza keeps the keys to Herod's quarters."

"Where?"

Her eyes dropped to the floor. "When he doesn't have them in hand, they are hanging on the wall in the accounting room."

The two men smiled at each other. What they had suspected was now confirmed. Chuza held the keys to most of the rooms.

"We made good progress in mapping out the many hallways and corridors at the palace, but there are a few hidden passageways we have not yet discovered. We're thinking that your husband must know the locations of these. Perhaps you can enlighten us. How can we utilize them, to access important areas like the treasury?"

"You say the people are important to you. However it seems all you are interested in is Herod's money."

"You are wrong, Joanna," Namen contended, "We are interested in the people... The citizens of Galilee; and the people who should be in power, not the ones who are presently in power."

He stood with his arms crossed, rocking back and forth from heel to heel, with an impish grin on his face.

Occasionally he gestured with open hand towards his opponent, as though offering an uncontested truth. He laughed as he spoke.

"You think you have the answer for Galilee? Let me tell you what the answer is..." He leaned back now as he spoke. "The answer is less taxes, and better men in power!"

The man continued to rock back and forth, which Joanna found more annoying than anything. Had he no idea how stupid he looked? Here was Namen, trying to persuade her with the charm of an idiot. No, she had enough of that with Herod!

"We are hoping to divert the marriage of Neodius to Herodius' daughter, since that would hinder our cause."

Of course that's it, Joanna realized. That marriage would strengthen Herod's power and annex Seleucia under Herod's authority, and under his taxation! How did she not understand it before? They wanted Herod's power weakened, not strengthened!

"I see even Herod appreciates some Parthian treasures. Those deep blue vases near the entrances? Well, they come from the glorious land of Parthia, my dear."

"Impressive," Joanna said blandly.

"Herod doesn't appear to get up early, does he?" Namen continued. "But he is punctual. He rises every morning at precisely the third hour. Very predictable I must say, and that will be a great benefit to our cause."

Ephraim now cut in, "We must inform the common people what Rome is about. Herod has master-minded a system of control to which everyone measures up. If they don't, Herod sends one of his henchmen to take care of the smallest uprisings." Ephraim lifted his eyebrows as he spoke. His arms were constantly on the move, gesturing to maximize his arguments.

Joanna moved to the side, "Herod is no dumb person. He acts dumb, but he is a skilled leader."

Namen stepped back, his hand resting on his chin, and his index finger stroking the side of his nose. "I heard he made quite a scene in the hallway of the palace just the other day." Again, he grinned as he spoke.

Joanna rubbed her two big toes back and forth as they itemized the times at which the guards changed, the details of each day's menu, and dozens of other tidbits of seemingly useless information. *They're letting me know they have gathered sufficient information to invade the palace,* she calculated to herself.

The two men began to describe every corner of Herod's palace, and each person's responsibilities. After what seemed like endless chatter about Herod and his schedules, both men stopped for a moment, and sat back down. They looked directly at Joanna and restated their point. This time it was Ephraim who spoke.

"We must be able to trust you. We have collected much information, but we need someone who can arrange situations, move certain people in and out, and cause diversions."

Joanna nodded hesitantly, becoming somewhat afraid of their implications.

The man went on, "You know one of Herod's most trusted men, Plouton. We want you to continue to cooperate with him, but time is urgent. We needed you to get those approvals with the seal of Herod, but you were off in Rome! Perhaps you had no choice in the matter, but understand your trip held us up considerably. When you get back to Tiberias, your first job is to get those documents sealed."

He continued, "What is at stake here is the freedom of every man and woman of Galilee, Judea, and even

Jerusalem. The people have been slaves to the laws of Caesar and Herod for too long. We believe you are in a position to help us finalize the overthrow of Herod."

This was the first time Joanna heard them use the term overthrow, and she carefully weighed the word. It sounded military. It was not an economic term. It described warfare.

"You told us your husband holds the keys to Herod's quarters. What about the keys to the other rooms of the palace?"

"Most of them." Joanna knew that Herod would never allow any one person to hold exclusive access to the treasury. She also knew that Chuza had more access than anyone else at the palace, and figured the Parthians may have guessed that.

"The keys with their locks," Joanna began, "are not like an average householder's. The hasps are loaded with springs, and the keys must be fully inserted and compressed. Then you lift it up to release the pin. If you are familiar with Egyptian key and lock systems, you will have no problem figuring out how to work the Roman ones. They are very similar."

The men asked Joanna to draw diagrams of how the locks worked, and then asked her to clarify several details. "This is valuable information. Yes, I think we understand how to work these locks now."

The men then began to drill her with questions about Chuza. "Does he meet with Herod? How often? Would you be able to get some keys for us?"

Joanna explained to them the things she was sure of, occasionally glancing up to see their expressions. There weren't any expressions. They were trained military leaders, intent on collecting information like it was the greatest jewel of worth. They leaned forward on their chairs, peering at Joanna like she was perhaps yet withholding some small morsel of information from them. At times their voices raised slightly, and Namen, the smaller, less-dressed man grasped the handle on his sword as he interrogated her further. This was no fooling matter. Joanna felt the palms of her hands getting sweaty. She tried not to reveal the slight tremble in her knees. How can two men be so friendly one day, and so cold the next, she asked herself. They could dance with her, and they could beat her. She now realized they might even injure her. Or kill me, she told herself. If she didn't lose her life at the hands of over-exuberant Parthians, she could certainly be killed by Herod himself if he ever found out. She shuddered at the thought.

Ephraim, the taller man was more the statesman. He kind of reminded her of Chuza, she thought, whereas Namen was obviously more of a field soldier, perhaps finding his way up the Parthian political ladder. Namen was also younger, but that only made him more energetic and forceful in his speech. "We think if we can control the economics of Herod, we can control the nation of Herod. We must use utmost care in understanding everything about that man. He is a suspicious and cruel animal."

Again, Joanna nodded. She couldn't agree more.

"He is a meticulous collector of taxes, utilizing publicans everywhere to rob the civilians."

Joanna held her approval. Herod was an animal, but her husband was the steward of all taxation. She stopped short of agreeing that Chuza was a 'robber'.

Encouraged by the boldness of Namen, Ephraim now continued, "As Parthians we understand the importance of supporting the nation's workers. We value allegiance to the farmer, and the working man. We may not have the skill and equipment of the Romans, but we have our dignity."

He stood up. He looked down at Joanna, still crouching uncomfortably on the chair, and waved his hand inches from her face. He lowered his voice, "Herod trusts only Chuza. That may be a good thing, or not. But we do have a problem—he is your husband."

The man allowed the silence that followed to accentuate the point.

Joanna, however, knew what they wanted to hear. She quickly justified that lying was the easiest way to get out of a tight spot, and she could do it without the slightest twitch. Whatever they wanted to hear, that is what she would tell them.

"My husband gets what he wants in bed. Beyond that, I actually hate him. The way he accommodates Herod! He's disgusting! No. You don't have to worry about Chuza. He might as well be dead now!"

Joanna had obviously done a good job of convincing them. The men grinned at the passion with which she spoke. They both stood up, and prepared to pay her.

She looked at the coins in his hand. "Forty denarii?"

"That is the agreed amount."

Joanna could be as feisty as a cornered cat when things didn't go the way she wanted. "You told me my payment would be four thousand denarii!" she screamed.

They would pay her! One way or another! And for the first time in a long time, she seriously doubted the motives of the Parthian empire.

"No, we said 'forty,'" they insisted.

"You said if I helped you, I would receive a hundred times that amount!"

"But there is so much help we still need from you!"

She glared at them in astonishment. Joanna grabbed the forty denarii from his hand, and stomped toward the door, furious.

But both Ephraim and Namen stopped her. Namen pulled a small sword from its sheath, a stabbing sword about a half-cubit in length, made for close combat, and held it in front of Joanna's face.

Joanna froze!

"You will help us, or you will be treated as our enemy," he lowered his voice to a growl, "and you know what happens to Parthian enemies!"

Chapter Fourteen

Questions

"Forty Denarii!" Joanna exclaimed defiantly to Mary as she recalled the morning's encounter with Ephraim and Namen.

"Surely they will pay you what they promised," Mary defended.

"I don't believe it! I don't trust them."

"But Namen…"

"Namen is not who you think he is, Mary. He threatened me with his sword! So kind at the party! So cruel otherwise!"

"Joanna!" Mary exclaimed in terrible surprise.

But Joanna was unmoved, and although she softened her voice, she insisted, "Well I thought you would want to know... Anyway, I have no choice. I have to cooperate with Parthia. So guess where that leaves me with Chuza."

"Maybe you should talk to Chuza. He might cooperate with the Parthians."

Mary touched a nerve with Joanna, and Joanna glared at Mary as she spoke, "Chuza will never defect to Parthia! And I wouldn't either if I had a choice. But I'm not going to put my head on the block just to show loyalty to Rome."

"Namen was only trying to scare you, Joanna," Mary inserted, "he really wouldn't harm you."

"No," Joanna stated emphatically, "they were ready to kill me on the spot if I didn't cooperate. I know it!"

Mary shook her head in disbelief.

Mary changed the subject. "I've been thinking about lots of things, Joanna... lots about my life, my heart."

"Sounds serious," Joanna responded.

"I've never given much thought to religion, but... Do you remember the Galilean teacher, Joanna?"

"Who? Jesus? We were both there..."

"I stopped to listen to him awhile the other day. Something about Jesus captivates me. He's not like other men. No, when he speaks... I don't know... I like him."

"What do you mean? Did you become his disciple?"

"No, not yet. But I think I could. While I was listening to him, it was like... like I was being stirred inside, spiritually." she explained.

Joanna stood to her feet, and shuffled across the floor. "This Jesus must be some man! But Mary, be careful. You and he might end up dead like one of those other rebels."

Mary laughed, "Jesus, a rebel? Some of the Jews call him their king, so he might be a threat to Herod. But he doesn't operate like a rebel—more like a prophet. Anyway, you don't have to worry, Joanna. I'm not his disciple yet. Those disciples of his are quite strange."

"So if you become his disciple, that would make you quite strange too, wouldn't it?"

Mary laughed again and nodded, understanding the connection. "Don't worry. I'm not ready to become His disciple, at least not yet," she stated.

Joanna had a lot of other things to talk about. Chuza's work schedule seemed endless. Herod's antics made for good humor any day. Crabolus had aggravated her on numerous occasions. The most recent was her encounter with the Parthian spies right there in Magdala. She couldn't get away from that subject. She wasn't used to being taken advantage of, and the meager forty denarii jingled in her pocket like cheap toys.

"Mary, I just remembered something I was told in Jerusalem!"

"What in Caesar's name are you talking about?"

"Matus—You said you met him once, that he's friends with Ephraim and Namen. He's from Parthia, and I now remember something he said to me!"

"OK, Joanna!" Mary sighed, "What did this Matus say to you?"

"His exact words were, 'Even if those taxes were not removed, but just lowered slightly'. Mary, the Parthians aren't planning on removing taxes! They want to take over our country! I don't trust them." Joanna's words trailed off in misery.

Mary slid her hand forward, and rapped her finger on the wooden table in front of Joanna. "Now Joanna, I've spent a lot of time discussing this with Namen, and he has told me many times how there will be great benefits for all us Galileans."

"Well, that's not the way I see it. First Matus, now Ephraim's forty denarii, and who knows what's next."

"Don't be so pessimistic. Things will work out," Mary muttered, not willing to argue the point further.

By the time they had covered most of the concerns of their lives, all the lamps shining from nearby homes had long been extinguished. The sun had set hours ago, and finally the lamp on their table burned its last, flickered and died.

They stumbled their way in the dark, each to a bed, and threw themselves on the beds, exhausted from the day, yet content to be in the same house together. Friends like this were very special, and Joanna knew she would be friends with Mary for life, regardless of Jesus, Herod, or the Parthians.

The next morning, Joanna and Mary worked together at the tasks of preparing the morning meal, and then cleaning up. When done, they exchanged glances, and it was almost as if they could read each other's mind.

"Umm... Would you be interested in going down to Capernaum today?" Mary began.

Already knowing the reason why Mary wanted to go, Joanna played ignorant.

"...And why would you want to go to Capernaum today?" she asked in a rising voice, mocking the silliness of the question.

"Just to see someone..."

"And this someone... Is he possibly the teacher Jesus?"

"Possibly," Mary said, and smiled from the corner of her mouth, giving another quick glance to Joanna.

Joanna was about to say no, but laughed instead. "I suppose it wouldn't hurt anything. Anyway, I can't go back to Tiberias right now. My head might be at stake." She shrugged her shoulders, pulled her coat on, and the two of them headed out the door.

Mary tried not to show it, but she was pleased her best friend had, for the first time, chosen to accompany her on such a 'Jesus' adventure.

"What a terrific day!" Mary grinned. Indeed it was. A gentle breeze moved off the lapping waves of the Sea of Galilee, giving the air a refreshing humidity mingled with the scent of many flowers growing along the path. Migrating birds flew in large flocks, moving across the sky in synchronized harmony.

"Can you slow down a bit, Mary? Just because you can outrun me, doesn't mean you have to! We're not in a race are we?"

Mary laughed, "I guess my enthusiasm grew out my feet!" She slowed up to a more normal pace, but a few minutes later the pace quickened again."

"I give up!" Joanna panted, "Can we stop and rest here?"

"Alright, I'll walk slower."

Just then Mary grabbed Joanna's arm and pointed ahead.

"What?" Joanna demanded.

"There! Behind those bushes I saw something move!"

Joanna instantly thought of the last encounter they had had with robbers in the hills outside Tiberias. Not again! She huddled close to Mary and stared at the large bush beside the road. Joanna had no doubt about it. She too had seen something!

"Let's go back!" Mary whispered.

At that instant the air erupted with a thunderous noise as hundreds of crested larks flapped their wings out of the bush and headed directly over the heads of Mary and Joanna.

Both of them screamed at the same time. They collapsed to the ground, covering their heads with their arms, as the army of birds fluttered noisily but harmlessly above them. Joanna screamed again. This time she grabbed a stick and waved it above her head.

"Get away!"

The two women kicked their feet in the air, like they expected a deadly avian attack. But obviously the flock of birds now had double reason to leave. Within seconds they were gone, flapping their wings furiously along the sea shore for a destination more restful.

Mary and Joanna lay stunned on the ground for a moment, and then burst with uncontrolled laughter! How incredibly silly they looked. They both leaned on an elbow and stared at each other, a gaggle of two, barely able to catch their breath, but hooting all the while!

"Stupid birds!" Joanna rasped.

Mary caught sight of a couple with children in the distance behind them. "People are coming, Joanna! Get up!" A traveling family ambled down the road, coming toward them. The two women quickly got up, brushed the dirt off their garments, and started down the road in the direction of Capernaum.

"No need for anyone else to enjoy our embarrassment!" Mary chuckled again.

Chapter Fifteen

Jesus Teaches Simple Faith

The morning sun had begun to warm the air when Mary and Joanna arrived in Capernaum. Crowds had already gathered around Jesus. It was teaching time, and the masses didn't seem to mind standing quietly. They listened attentively to the prophet as he spoke:

"You must come to the kingdom with child-like faith.

"Don't be like the Pharisees.

"No one comes to the Father except through me.

"Out of the abundance of the heart, the mouth speaks."

Joanna listened intently while Jesus expounded on each point. When Jesus talked about child-like faith, all she could think of was her doubts about people like Jesus. When Jesus talked about the Pharisees, Joanna nodded her head with the rest of the crowd, while off in a corner the group of black-robed religious leaders stared at Jesus defiantly. And when Jesus talked about what was in people's hearts—all Joanna could think about was the corruption of her own life, and the feelings of despair and frustration she often held within her heart.

Jesus continued expounding on another point, "But I say to you that whoever looks at a woman to lust for her has already committed adultery with her in his heart."

I don't like it! She knew His point was also true for a woman. She had lusted. She had procured lusting in men. The teaching of Jesus was far too piercing for Joanna's soul. It cut her to the core of her heart. She tried to shrug off the impact of what Jesus had said, but His words echoed in her mind. The words of condemnation also rang in her head: Joanna—the lustful woman that you are!

Joanna shifted her feet, uncomfortably. She didn't like the excitement, the unexplainable miracles, and most of all, His discourse. But Jesus was animated, and now began to speak to various ones in the crowd, sometimes laying a hand on them. Many of them broke down and wept in remorse.

Now he picked up a child and was illustrating his point about child-like faith.

Joanna turned to Mary and asked, "What did Jesus mean when he said no one can come to the Father except through Him?"

"I think it's because the people recognize him as the Messiah, sent from the Father as God Himself."

"So people actually believe he is God's Son?"

"Just watch the miracles he does… Who else can do such things?" Mary replied.

No sooner had Mary spoken than a man passed by carrying his cot. He shouted excitedly, "I can walk! I am free!" Several of his family accompanied him as he made his way through the crowd. They too were shouting and laughing for joy.

Joanna stared at him as he passed by. Amazing!

Mary joined with the entire crowd by taking off her outer coat, and proceeded to wave it above her head, like a flag. Joanna swallowed. Her friend was deeper into this than she previously thought.

The muscles in Joanna's neck tensed and she held her arms tightly against her side. She wasn't about to join in! She looked at the ground, and tried not to respond to Mary's exuberance. But Mary kept bumping into her as she danced in circles.

"This is fanatical!" Joanna finally muttered, rather loudly.

Mary wore a smile as wide as a river! While still dancing around, she spoke back to Joanna, "I guess then..." She made another swirling turn, "that makes me..." and another full turn around and stopped squarely before Joanna, "a fanatic!" With that she threw both of her hands in the air, and gave a delightful squeal, jumping up and down several times.

Delightful, that was, to Mary and everyone else. But not to Joanna. She just wanted to get out of there. Here she was, trapped in a mob of maniacs, and who knows what they would do next!

"Look!" Mary cried out, and pointed. A father was running through the masses, carrying a child on his shoulders, yelling, "He was dead yesterday, but today he is alive! Jesus healed my boy!" Jesus' eyes met the man as he ran, and he smiled, "Blessings to you!"

Joanna glanced over at Mary. She didn't want to lose her friend. What would she do if Mary became one of his disciples?

A few hours later, Joanna and Mary made their way over to a local market and diner in Capernaum. There, they sat across from each other under the shade of olive trees. They had finished their lunch when a herald came down the street and passed the market.

"Hear the news!" the young man shouted as he entered the town's market square, "Danos has been invaded by the Parthians! Twenty-five Roman soldiers have been killed in the assault!"

Joanna and Mary looked up from the round stone table between them. The runner continued to call out to everyone along the street. In the diner, many of the guests began to chat excitedly about the news.

Joanna looked back at Mary. "Where is Danos?"

A woman sipping cider at a near table overheard Joanna's question and replied, "Danos is in Syria, near Mount Hermon... quite a fortress. I'm surprised Parthia was able to capture the town." She stopped short of expressing her favor to the Parthian cause, but her enthusiasm did not escape the two ladies either.

"Sounds like she is happy about it," Joanna whispered to Mary. Mary nodded in agreement.

"Danos is a long way from here," Joanna tried to convince herself, shaking her head; "they won't invade us." Joanna bit her lower lip in concern. What if the Parthians did invade Tiberias! She thought about the people living in Danos. They probably didn't expect to be invaded. The Parthians were surely persistent. Perhaps a Parthian invasion of Galilee was more likely than she supposed. But she dare not believe it.

At that moment another customer took up the topic with his friend. "I think it's highly unlikely the Parthians will invade us here in Capernaum. No, we're too far south for that."

His friend nodded, "...but it might be not so bad, you know. This country needs a change."

"True, but we do have good security with Rome. Anyway, they've tried before and failed. Remember back — what was it — maybe thirteen years ago. Rome sent them scurrying back home like rats to the river!"

"Yes, but that was under a different Herod. He killed off his own family to keep power. Our Herod Antipas seems more of a joke to me."

His friend nodded.

Joanna remarked to Mary, "It seems Galileans pick their favorites."

"Yes," said Mary, "but with a lot of caution. They have to make sure they give only enough allegiance to be safe should either side win the war."

Mary picked up her cup of cider, and looked straight at Joanna. "Danos may be a long way north, but don't forget, this entire region is already greatly influenced by Parthians."

"Like Ephraim and Namen!" Joanna scowled.

"You really have a dislike for those two men, don't you? You should give them a chance. You might surprise yourself."

Chapter Sixteen

Suspicious Activity at the Palace

Back in Tiberias, Chuza made his way down the hallway to the key lockup. The sun had set a good hour earlier, and now the dim flicker of the lamps cast eerie shadows along the corridor walls. It only made sense, he reasoned, that the most secure devices be kept close to Herod's personal quarters. Unfortunately for Chuza, he had to ramble down the darkened hallways, and the sound of his feet echoed mysteriously from the stone floor. He had done the task hundreds of times before, and knew the routine well. However, the sound still irked him. Chuza quickened his pace. With uninvited guests lurking about the courtyards, and the rumors of impending treason abounding, he couldn't be too careful.

He looked down at the keys in his hands, and, arriving at his destination, inserted the keys against the compression springs. He gave them a turn, and slid the hasp over to free the door. Having completed his mission, he reversed the operation, and headed back.

I can't wait to be home, Chuza thought.

Just as he passed by the last junction he thought he saw something moving down a side hallway to the left. Or was it? He couldn't quite tell, and stopped to stare down the corridor, but nothing moved further. At the first he was almost sure he had seen something. Now there was nothing. He tried to dismiss it, but couldn't. Something or someone had been there, perhaps watching him putting the keys away!

Chuza decided to double check his suspicions. He took two steps away from the hallway junction, then stopped and listened. Nothing. He quietly moved back to the junction, and peered around the corner to where he first thought he had seen something. Still nothing. He would get a couple of guards to check down the hallway later.

He took only a few steps when suddenly a horrendous crash sounded from the very place he had previously looked. Chuza jumped and turned in fright. The skin on his arms, legs, and neck shriveled into goose bumps. He drew his sword, and held it out in front as he rushed back to the junction. He peered down the side hallway again, and the figure of a large man lay crumpled in the center of the floor. In front of him were the remains of a broken jug of wine.

"Crabolus! You stupid drunk fool!" Chuza roared, "what in Caesar's kingdom are you doing?"

"I tripped," Crabolus stuttered.

"I have in mind to run you through with my sword, and that is what you deserve!"

Crabolus laughed in mockery, wiping his hand across his drooling mouth, "Then who is going to warn Herod?"

Chuza grabbed him by the arm, and hoisted him up, ignoring the absurdity of Crabolus' comment. He was about to help him walk along the hallway, when another thought struck him. What if Crabolus was not alone?

"Wait here," Chuza commanded. With that he half threw him against the side wall, where he again collapsed to the floor.

Chuza turned and checked each room carefully along the corridor. Convinced Crabolus was alone in his mischief, he returned, and dragged him out of the area. Once he reached the guards, he instructed them to take him home immediately, and then get the servants to clean up the whole mess on the hallway floor.

Chapter Seventeen

The Storm

Joanna tried to think of a way to get from Magdala back to Tiberias unnoticed. The Parthians had given her an ultimatum: Either cooperate or have her long held secret revealed. It left her frustrated and fearful. She didn't want to risk the Parthians bullying her on the way home, or even spying on her.

My life is a life of frustrations, she thought to herself. She had been living loosely, and wondered if the Parthians had been spying on her all along, and knew of her secret sins.

She hated herself at times like this. She hated the first encounter she had had with wayfaring strangers in Magdala, not realizing, until after, that they were affiliated with the Parthian cause. Truth was, she shouldn't have gotten involved with them in the first place.

Now she had a dilemma; either provide them the information, or they would tell Chuza what his wife was really up to. She knew the consequence of adultery. Stoning.

Joanna carefully walked to the edge of Magdala. She intentionally strolled with a casual saunter, but her eyes darted side to side, and behind her. No one seemed to be following. She took to the road out of town, leading toward home.

The mixture of humidity from the lake, and the hot sun burning down, made the air sultry. By mid-afternoon, the clouds had billowed over the Galilean shores. The clouds building increased the possibility of rain before she could make Tiberias. A shower might be in the works, but she didn't expect a large storm. That is, until she rounded the top of a hill bordering Galilee and could see the waves across the sea churning a dull grey-green color. Whitecaps were everywhere! On the slopes up from the shoreline, a dust squall moved rapidly toward her. She realized she was in trouble.

The rolling black cloud advanced, kicking up dirt and small stones. Now the rolling cloud turned into a swirling wind, spinning with the force of a hurricane. If she turned back, she would run straight into it. She broke into a run toward Tiberias, but within minutes it was upon her. When the wind hit, an unexpected gust from the side caught her off balance. She tried to brace herself, but before she could do so, the blast knocked her off her feet. She slammed into a thorn bush off the side of the path.

Joanna screamed! The dirt stirred up by the wind stung her face. She squeezed her eyes shut to keep out the churning dust. She lay helpless, pressed by the howling wind against the thorns that scratched her face, and stabbed her legs, arms and buttocks. For a full three minutes the storm beat upon her, and then hail began to pelt down. At first only a few pieces of ice fell, but then the hail intensified in both numbers and size. Every time one hit her head, it felt like her skull would crack, and she yelped. Then the hail turned into a driving rain, soaking her from top to bottom.

Finally the wind began to die, and she struggled to free herself from the tangled barbs of the thorn bush. She opened her eyes as best she could, her eyelids now stained with dark brown dirt mixed with blood and tears.

Joanna sobbed uncontrollably. Her wet and clinging dress was tattered by the thorns. When she tried to pull herself out of the bush, several thorns caught her clothing, gashing both cloth and skin. She stomped her feet in anger, and plodded up the path toward home.

Looking down at what used to be a nice clean dress and gown, she grunted again. Why me? With that, she regained some of her composure, and stormed up the hill.

As quickly as the storm had come, it went. The storm clouds were now swept away by the wind, and piled high against the hills beyond Tiberias. The sun peeked out, and a rainbow glowed in the eastern sky.

So much for these clothes! she thought. Oh well—good thing Chuza is rich. She consoled herself several times by thinking of getting a new wardrobe. Afterward, she felt calmed. She then amused herself by comparing her life to the storm. She looked at her clothes, all stained with brown streaks from the dirt.

"Yes," she said out loud, "that's my life. A terrible storm! And my clothes—Yes, that's my tattered life!" She gritted her teeth at the truth of the statement, but managed a short smile at her self-amusing wit.

The more she thought about the comparison, the less panicky she became. Now that she was clear minded, she renewed her resolve. She wasn't going to give up, but something had to change. Somehow she would break free from her Parthian hook. She just had to!

Chuza once told her she was the most determined woman he had ever met. She proved him right on most accounts. Determination got her into trouble, and it would be the thing to get her out of trouble. How, she did not know.

For a moment, she considered what Mary had said about the prophet Jesus. Mary seemed to be quite impressed with the miracles and speech of Jesus, and talked to her often about the man. Mary had been drawn in by a unique spiritual force. Joanna had noticed some changes in Mary's life as well. She didn't throw herself in total abandonment at any man. Even her speech had sweetened. Joanna reached for a reason. Perhaps Mary was more desperate than her. That, in her desperation, Mary had pursued her spirituality. Whatever the motive, the changes in Mary seemed to stick. She even became defensive when, the odd time, Joanna ridiculed her for contacting Jesus so often. It was a clear indication how Mary cared for the "Jesus religion" passionately.

Joanna quickly assured herself she was not that desperate. I can fix my own problems, Joanna resolved, as she topped the hill, and fixed her eyes on the city of Tiberias on the horizon. Mary had debated the fact with her just a week ago. "You can't fix yourself," she had said, and although Joanna suspected it to be true, she wasn't about to accept it. At least not yet.

The next day, she noticed Plouton was on guard at the palace. She remembered what the Parthians had told her, and strolled up to meet him.

"We need to get together soon," she said in hushed tones as she passed by.

Plouton followed her along the wall, to a place beyond the ears of the others.

"Did you get the seal?" he asked.

"We must do it differently. I will get caught for sure if I take Herod's seal, even for a day. No, you get the documents to me, and I will seal them in Chuza's office."

Plouton understood, and agreed to the plan.

"Oh, I actually have two more needing the seal."

"That makes four, but four is more than we agreed upon. When will I receive payment?"

"I had hoped to receive my payment by now, but it will be here soon. Meanwhile, we must get those documents sealed. I will meet you back here in exactly one hour."

"I won't forget."

An hour later, Plouton was already waiting when Joanna walked over to receive the documents for the four pending guards. She looked at the names: Domitianus, Gnaeus, Theon, and Crabolus. Crabolus!

"Crabolus!" she whispered loudly, "He's already in the palace!"

"As a food and service butler, but not as a guard," replied Plouton. "Crabolus needs to have access to every part of the palace. He goes everywhere, but also gets in trouble for it too. As a guard, no one will question him wherever he goes!"

"How convenient!" Joanna mocked. "Honestly, Plouton, how can you even want someone like Crabolus as a guard?"

"I understand your concern, but a man like Crabolus will do anything to get an advantage. He is not bound in fear like most. He'll even make a fool of himself to find success!"

"I can't do it!" Joanna stated, recalling her many terrible encounters with Crabolus yelling at her.

"But you have no choice, Joanna." Plouton lowered his voice, "Either you get these four documents sealed, or I will tell Chuza that you slept with me."

Joanna resigned herself to the fact that she would have to complete the mission. But she didn't want to leave empty handed either.

Joanna re-stated her position. "You offered to pay me for getting these documents sealed."

"I just told you! I hoped to be paid by now, but I haven't. I assure you — the moment I receive my funds, you will certainly get your portion. We must cooperate in this venture. And don't worry so much. I won't be talking to Chuza — unless, of course, you fail in this task!"

Joanna knew Plouton was dead serious. She reluctantly took the parchments, rolled them up, and tucked them in her halug. She moved off into the palace to finish the job.

Chapter Eighteen

John the Baptist Imprisoned

A horn blew announcing the weekly 'speaker's forum' in Herod's court. Joanna turned instinctively to see the gates open, and was surprised when hundreds of people entered the courtyard.

"It's John the Baptist!" she overheard several bystanders say. Indeed he was. Unbelievably, he was the very same man she had seen preaching to the crowds along the Jordan River during her trip to Jerusalem.

This John the Baptist has become quite a popular attraction! she thought. She then quickly reminded herself not to be too surprised, since John had already been summoned by Herod several times before. Herod seemed to have a personal liking for John. Or, perhaps Herod was simply entertained by the appearance of another madman like himself. Joanna chuckled at the thought.

At least he dressed like one. John wore the same piece of leather wrapped about his waist, and the same camel skin cloak. Certainly no one would forget the man once they had met him. His appearance was one thing, but he was a good talker too. In a society where the best speakers had the greatest influence, John could hold his own in any forum. He spoke with conviction, and could waggle his finger quicker than Herod to make a point; that being no small achievement.

But while Herod seemed to be a permanent hunchback, John stood straight up, shoulders back, and stared in the eyes of those to whom he preached. Herod, on the other hand, invoked fear in others by his unpredictable tantrums, and could throw a chair across the room in an instant. But his eyes only left the floor to squint half sideways at his adversaries. Statesman he was not, but inquisitive of just about everything, and had become a knowledgeable student as a result.

Joanna moved away from the table where she had been sitting, and followed the crowd into the courtroom. As usual, King Herod sat on his throne, with the guest now seated below and off to the side. The heat of the afternoon made standing with the large crowd unpleasantly sticky. Joanna waited near the back of the crowd, where she could at least get an arm's length distance from the nearest person. She took the opportunity to observe who else was present. Crabolus, who couldn't miss any event, paced like a hyena from one entry to another. She recognized others too, from townspeople to royalty, all having a curious interest in this man.

Her eyes shifted to the other side of the throne. There stood Herod's new wife, Herodias, accompanied by her daughter, Salomis, and other members of her family. Herodias was finely decked in a long flowing gown, overly adorned by gems that sparkled in the sunlight. She protruded her chin in a haughty way, giving anyone that passed by too closely a quick reprove with the thrust of her nose. Joanna couldn't help but think of the uproar Herod had made six months ago, when he visited his brother Philip, tetrarch to the north, and returned with a new wife—Philip's wife none the less! "Stolen right from under his nose," the people had said.

Chuza appeared at Joanna's side for a moment, more to check on the behavior of the crowd than out of interest to hear John.

"Isn't he the fellow we met at the Jordan River on our Jerusalem trip?"

"The very man," Joanna replied, "wearing the same clothes."

Chuza sniffed the air, "Can't tell if it's him, or just all the people here on a hot day! Anyways, I hate crowds." With that, he left as suddenly as he had appeared.

The trumpet blew again, longer this time, indicating the session was about to begin. The crowd became silent as they shuffled to better positions to view the speaker of the day.

Herod raised his crooked arm. "Welcome to the speaker's forum—a time for me to enlighten my mind, and entertain my heart! Today the prophet John is here. I have many questions to ask of John today. At our last encounter, he seemed quite convinced that God was about to judge all the people of earth, and everyone needed repentance—even a peaceful soul like mine!"

The crowd, many who were disciples of John, choked off their laughter at the absurdity of Herod being a peaceful soul.

"Your name is quite intriguing," Herod began, "John—the Baptist. People get baptized because they give allegiance to a cause they believe in."

"There is no greater cause than God," John stated without hesitation.

Herod leaned over, smiling crookedly; his rounded shoulders making his enormous head look even more peculiar. "You should baptize for Caesar," he laughed, "then you would be doing something for our country! So why do you baptize? I can't understand for a moment why you think it is so important for people to go through this... ritual." He waved his arm outward as he attempted to define what he didn't understand.

"Herod, baptism is what people do to demonstrate true repentance."

"Oh, yes. Repentance! We have found your favorite topic once again."

For the next quarter hour Herod quizzed John about baptism traditions, and then asked him about a rumor.

"Is it true you eat locusts to stay alive?" Without giving John time to respond, Herod grinned and made another off-handed remark about his diet. "I don't know another man in the kingdom who lives under a rock, and eats insects with wild honey to stay alive!"

Even though Herod was quite curious about peculiarities of dress and diet, his main interest always lay in politics. And, of course, Herod's real intent was to discern if John's preaching was a threat to his power. That knowledge was well beyond curiosity. It was vital to Herod's control of Galilee, and thus vital to his favor with Caesar. So he now addressed John directly, "I am interested in what you say, John. What does God's law and Caesar's law have in common? John, please answer this question for us."

Joanna

The 'leather and camel-skin man' left the chair where he was sitting and stood at an angle in front of Herod. He spoke loudly and with conviction. "With God there is no difference between Caesar and the poorest servant. God is judge of them both. They both will need to repent to escape the judgment of…"

"Why then," Herod interrupted, "should anyone obey a God they cannot see? Would it not make more sense to obey Caesar who is our very visible king, and our worshipped leader? After all, I don't see God appearing with a sword to vindicate his enemies!"

"The day will come," John jumped in without hesitation, "when God will judge everyone. Those who have lived a life of drunkenness will be judged. Those who commit adultery will be judged. Those who steal and lie will be judged. Those who…"

"Yes, yes," Herod sighed, "I have heard this all before. You think I am a sinner…" He suggested the question with the same defensive grumble in his voice.

"You are what you are. Let me ask you this question, King Herod: Do you live by the law of God?"

Herod was defiant in his answer, "No! Of course I don't live by the law of God. I live by the law of Caesar just as I have said!" He paused for a few seconds. "Your 'law of God' forbids drunkenness?"

"Yes it does, and the law also forbids marrying another man's wife."

Herod's face turned red, and his voice reached a new growl, "You! You are accusing me?"

John didn't have to answer. The crowd took up the case with many religious people shouting out the fact that Herod had stolen his brother Philip's wife.

From across the court, Herod's new wife Herodias slammed her foot on the floor, and spat in the direction of

John. "You'll pay for this, you devil!" she muttered, and stormed out of the courtroom.

"I gave you the privilege to come and speak of your religion here in my court, and now you are accusing me and my wife! What do you say, John? Is it not lawful for Herodias to be my wife?"

"God's law says you must be faithful to one wife. To marry another is to commit adultery."

"Enough already!" Herod yelled, "Get the man out of here!"

The forum had begun respectably, but now it ended abruptly and in anger. But as quickly as Herod had given the command, he thought again, and re-directed his guards, "Hold it! Guards! Do not let this man go. I have another plan! Put him in prison! We'll see if there is a law that can release him from that!"

The guards were upon John the Baptist in an instant, and pulled him out of the court, and towards the prison.

Together with the crowd, Joanna gasped! Imprisonment? Just for speaking honestly about what you believe? And that, at the request of Herod himself! Joanna turned to hide her disgust, and fled to her home.

Matthew 14:3 "For Herod had laid hold of John and bound him, and put him in prison for the sake of Herodias, his brother Philip's wife."

Chapter Nineteen

Mary on the Run

The sun had long disappeared behind the Galilean hills when Joanna arrived at the guest quarters just down the street at Tiberias. Joanna expected Mary would be waiting for her, and they would talk for hours as usual. Joanna would tell her about the incident with John the Baptist and Herod. She would tell her about Plouton, and the spies at the palace. Perhaps Mary would have some ideas on how she should handle the situation. She looked forward to visiting with her. So much had been happening; she needed the listening ear, and the caring soul which Mary provided. Lately Joanna felt a growing discontent. Hopefully talking with Mary might give her a plan to get out the mess she was in.

Even more than the discontent, Joanna felt like a traitor. She had disclosed information to Parthian spies which might endanger the palace, her husband, and perhaps the entire state of Judea. Between her encounter with Matus in Jerusalem, and what she had told Ephraim and Namen, they had almost enough to guarantee a successful invasion of the palace.

The darkening shadows of houses along the dusty street matched her inner fears. She wrapped her shawl around her neck as cold air forced its way across her face. Mary would update her on the Parthian force, good or bad. And Mary was still her friend, even if she had Parthians for companions and Jesus as her prophet or whoever he was. Friends were friends, and she was looking forward to a hot drink or perhaps even a bowl of sizzling lamb.

But she was disappointed as she neared the guest house. No lamp burned within, and Mary was not there.

Since Mary had not given any indication of going somewhere, Joanna simply opened the door and entered. She searched for a note explaining where she might be. Mary wouldn't be out bartering for grocery items at the town gate. The sky was already dark. She didn't have a lot of friends in Tiberias, so Joanna didn't think she was out visiting. And today was the middle of the week—highly unlikely for her to get hooked up with one of her soldier men.

She checked the table and counter in the food preparation area. Other than a few old parchments with some directions on them, she didn't find a note anywhere.

"I suppose I'll just wait." Joanna lit the lamp on the table, sat down on a simple wooden chair next to the table, and watched out the window.

She didn't have to wait long. Moments later, the door burst open with a bang, and Mary stumbled inside.

"You're drunk!" Joanna exclaimed.

Mary fell on one knee, her clothes tattered from multiple falls, and her legs and arms scratched and bruised. Mary's eyes darted from side to side, wide with fright, like a trapped animal! Then she screamed.

Joanna jumped to her feet. "Mary!"

She breathed in short, gasping breaths. Her chest heaved and she coughed steadily. She wildly paced back and forth, tripping over anything in her path.

"It's me... Me... Joanna!" She embraced Mary, hoping to settle her down.

But Mary tore away from Joanna, yelling, "It's going to get me! Don't let it get me!"

Once again, Joanna tried to calm her down, "Please Mary! Mary, please! It's OK. You've been drinking too much."

Mary shook her head. "No. Not drunk. It's something else!" Mary said. "It's trying to kill me!"

Joanna again tried to clutch her arm, "Mary, Don't be silly! Nothing's trying to kill you. Here, sit down," Joanna motioned to the chair. She firmly grabbed her arm, and attempted to get her to the seat, but Mary refused, thrusting her shoulders from side to side. Now Joanna was in tears. "Please, Mary!" she cried. Joanna grasped Mary's wrists in her hands, "Mary, What is the matter? What is it?"

Mary again shook her head wildly, "I've got to find him. I've got to find him."

"Who, Mary, who?"

"Jesus! I've got to find him!" Mary kept repeating.

Joanna glanced out the window. The black of night had fallen. "Oh, no Mary, You can't go tonight. It's too late, and besides, he's a crazy man! Stay away from him. Look at you!"

"But Joanna, I need him!" Once again Mary yanked her arm fiercely out of Joanna's grasp and this time she darted out through the door. She ran into the dark street, and continued down the hill.

Joanna ran screaming after her. "Mary! Mary! Stop! Don't go!"

But she was no match for Mary. Mary ran faster, and doubled by this crazy hysteria, she disappeared within seconds into the thick dark night.

Joanna spent most of the night searching. She wandered up and down every street in Tiberias, hoping to find her huddled in some corner. At times she stopped and called out for her, but each time there was no answer. She stopped in at home, and relayed the incident with Chuza, who promised to tell the palace guards to be on the lookout for her. That he would do, but he wasn't about to help Joanna search for Mary in the middle of the night.

Joanna also walked in and around the palace. She woke the women servants in their quarters. Many of them, including Miriam and Chaya, volunteered to help Joanna in her search for Mary. They rubbed the sleep from their eyes, and followed her along the streets. They checked every place they could think of.

"Perhaps she went to the palace," Joanna suggested.

The group walked back to the court where the speaker's forum had been. They even searched outside the city wall across the rolling hills in the moonlit sky, hoping to see Mary somewhere, but to no avail.

Finally, Joanna sat on a bench, helpless. Her body and soul ached. What could have gripped Mary in such a short time, and made her into an insane maniac? Was it that madman, Jesus? Why was Mary so desperate to see him? Why had she not been able to help Mary? Several of the servants put their hands on Joanna's shoulders to comfort her.

Joanna's imagination thought only the worst. She pictured Mary, stuck in some thorn bush, just like she had been during the storm. She still remembered the pain and helpless feeling. She peered at every shadow along the streets. They each had the appearance of an unconscious body. In her mind, she saw Mary running wildly, and then flying off a cliff to her death. Did she perhaps take one of the soldier's spears and fall on it? Perhaps she lay somewhere, bleeding and hurt? If only it were daylight. Then she would have been able to follow her. Instead, all she knew was that Mary had run, crying something about needing to see Jesus.

Most of the night hours had gone by, and the servants returned to their sleeping rooms. Suddenly she remembered something Mary had said the day before. At the time, she had barely taken notice, because she often ignored Mary's comments about Jesus. Now she remembered what Mary had said. Jesus was going to be visiting each village near Tiberias these days. He would be returning to Capernaum the next day. That's it! Of course that's where Mary is heading! Capernaum!

She ran out to the fenced area where the horses were tethered for night. Selecting the first horse she came to, she led it through the gate onto the street. She gave her a quick pat on the neck, and mounted. Moments later she was moving as fast as her horse would allow on the dark path down the hill. She cared not that it was night. She clenched her teeth with determination, and pressed on, checking the side of the path in the moonlight to examine any shadow that might be Mary. She had a mission to do, and darkness would not stop her.

As she approached Magdala, the eastern sky was turning light with dawn. She quickly checked Mary's home in case she had gone there, but wasn't surprised when Mary was not there. She pressed on toward Capernaum, and by the time she saw the town in the distance, the sun peeked above the horizon. Now she could see, and she put the horse into a full gallop. Within minutes, she entered the fishing village of Capernaum.

What do I do now? she wondered to herself. An older woman swept the dirt from off the porch of her house. Joanna trotted over and asked her if she knew where Jesus could be.

"Isn't he that fanatic from Nazareth?" she responded, "I have no idea where he is, but ask Suzanna here." She motioned next door, where a modest woman about Joanna's age also did some early morning fix-ups at the front of her home.

Joanna called to her, "Have you heard about Jesus? Do you know where I can find him?"

"Oh, yes. I am about to go meet him myself. He is teaching the people at the far gate of the city. Just follow this street to the end."

The woman continued, "Are you one of his disciples?"

Joanna wrinkled her nose without responding, and, giving the horse a kick in the ribs, rushed down the street.

Joanna wasn't sure if Mary could have even reached Capernaum yet, but thought it might be possible. Knowing that Jesus was indeed in this city, gave Joanna added hope of finding her best friend. Maybe if she talks with this Jesus, she'll get her thinking straightened out.

The horse twitched as a piercing shriek filled the air from somewhere up ahead. Joanna urged it on.

Then Joanna saw where the sound came from. Just on the other side of the city gate, a group of people was gathering. There, in the middle of them stood Jesus, pointing down at a woman writhing on the ground. She had seen such a scene once before, and didn't care to see it again. But she just had to find out... Another shriek!

Six times the woman convulsed violently, until, just as Joanna rode up, the woman gave out a final shriek, and now lay motionless.

Joanna was horrified by what she saw. Mary! It is Mary!

She brought the horse to a stop, dismounted, and scrambled through the crowd to Mary's side. Mary wasn't moving. Joanna put one hand on her back, and looked up to see Jesus looking back at her. "What happened?" Joanna asked.

Jesus looked down at Joanna and Mary, then up at the anxious crowd. He calmly addressed them all, "This is Mary, of Magdala. She came here this morning tormented by seven devils. But now she is delivered from them all, and she will be my disciple."

The crowd cheered.

Meanwhile Joanna still crouched over Mary. She glanced up at Jesus. His eyes seemed to pierce right through her. She dared not look up again.

Moments later, Mary regained consciousness. Even though she lay in the middle of the road in a crumpled heap, she directed her eyes up to Jesus. "Jesus! Forgive me my sins!"

"You are forgiven, and you are free! Mary, you will never be the same!"

"May it be as you say, Jesus."

Tears welled up in Mary's eyes. She propped herself up on her knees, and looked back at him with eyes of thanksgiving. "I am at peace, Jesus. No longer will I seek for love anywhere else, for I have found the love of God in you!"

Jesus stooped, took her by the hand and lifted her up. Her body vibrated—a spiritual surge shooting through her body as Jesus lifted her. Strength came to her ankles and knees, and the peace did not leave. His forgiving eyes met hers, "Go and sin no more, Mary. You will be one of my disciples. Go and tell your friends what has happened to you. Teach them to follow me."

Jesus smiled at her, then focused once again at Joanna, and said, "You too will be my disciple."

Joanna, turned around to see who he spoke to, but no doubt the comment was meant for her. She tried to dismiss what she had heard, but couldn't keep a tear from forming in her eye.

Mary now noticed Joanna. For several minutes, Mary stretched her arms on Joanna's shoulders and said, "Joanna, You aren't going to believe this! I found him! And I'm free! I don't know exactly what happened, but this I know—I used to be bound by evil spirits, and now I am totally free! I can never again live the life I once lived. He told me I was going to be his disciple. Oh, Joanna, let's follow him!"

Joanna pushed off. A perplexed and hard-pressed smile etched Joanna's face as she listened to Mary. "Well, yes, that is very nice, Mary. I am so happy for you."

Mary appeared angelic. Her face glowed, and she just stared at Joanna, smiling like she had won the world. But for Joanna, this was an awkward silence. Neither spoke for what seemed an eternity.

Finally, Joanna took a deep breath and broke the silence, "So what happened to you last night anyway?"

Mary recounted the events of the night before. All night long she had run. She had stumbled and fallen many times. Each time, desperation made her get up and run again. When she had gotten to Magdala, she didn't even stop at her home, but continued running in the dark. By the middle of the dark night, she was still a long ways away, and all she had known was that Jesus was supposed to be near Capernaum somewhere.

She described a peculiar incident during her running to Capernaum. Next to the Sea of Galilee, she had seen a man in the night. She had fumbled for words, surprised to see someone in the dark. "I am looking for..."

The man had said, "You are looking for Jesus, aren't you?"

"Yes, I am," she had made out, astonished, and puffing with exhaustion.

"You will find him just outside Capernaum, sitting and teaching the people," the man had said, smiling, and pointing down the road.

Mary had nodded a quick thank you, and scurried down the path. When she had turned to offer a quick glance behind her, the man was gone. Disappeared. It had to have been an angel!

She had hurried down the trail toward the city. Up the hills, down the valleys, around the curves, and alongside the sea. She had finally reached Capernaum shortly after the break of day.

Mary had hurried through the town and, what seemed like only moments later, she had reached the other side. As she had rounded a corner, a crowd had gathered, and praises for Jesus erupted in the air. A man who had a withered hand had been healed and then ran ecstatically in circles yelling out "Look at my hand! It's completely healed!" She had neared the throng, and saw Jesus, sitting on a donkey. He had been performing miracle after miracle! Before Mary realized it, she had pushed her way through the crowd, and stood before him.

She had looked up at Jesus and he had faced her, his eyes meeting Mary's. At once, she had felt something stirring within her. At the moment Jesus had looked at her, there was a bone-crushing feeling deep inside that tore at her essence. She had sensed the up-rising of evil spirits within her. It was a force within her, holding and binding her. As this force was torn from her, she had collapsed to the ground, twisting and writhing in torment. She felt the torture repeated several times.

People had told her that Jesus had gotten off the donkey and walked to her. He had stood over her, pointed his finger at her, and had spoken not to Mary, but to the evil spirits within her, and commanded them to release their captive. One by one, with an evil shriek, the spirits had come out. The crowd had counted seven shrieks, and finally, Mary had just lain there, motionless on the ground. Finally, Mary said, she had regained consciousness at the moment Joanna arrived.

Now, Mary recounted to Joanna the feelings of her heart. She was overwhelmed by a new feeling of spiritual peace. For the first time in her life she felt free. She felt the satisfaction of seeing a man who truly loved and cared for her in a pure way. She felt at ease, and at peace. It was even a peace with—God! Surely this Jesus—he must be the Son of God!

Mary finished her account of what had happened but Joanna had nothing much to say about it.

Joanna secretly worried that Mary had become insane. She even wondered if she had fallen and hit her head on a rock. Or maybe all this panic and fear came as a result of too much drinking. She had heard of that happening to people. On the other hand, now she had finally found this Jesus prophet. It was hard to tell—perhaps Mary was indeed changed, and destined to be a disciple of Jesus.

Joanna immediately set her defenses up as she recalled the many things her other friends had told her about Jesus: "Stay away from that kook! He is totally insane. People follow him because he claims to do miracles. I think he must be a magician or something."

"I wouldn't go near him!" one of her friends had said, and Joanna agreed. There was more to life than running after weird people. There was a life to be lived—parties to attend, and she certainly would not let herself entertain the idea of following someone as extreme as this Jesus. "I won't go near him!" she repeated to herself out loud.

In the afternoon, Mary followed Jesus as he moved to the next village. Joanna, relieved but still perplexed, mounted her horse, and made a somewhat lonely trip back to Tiberias.

What happened four days later caused Joanna to once again weigh the legitimacy of Jesus against other's opinions of him.

Joanna heard that Mary had arrived in Tiberias, and was looking for her. She immediately headed to the guest house to meet her. She hustled down the street, but before she could to reach the house, a young lady approached her, bouncing along with hair flowing behind her. Joanna stopped and stared. She looked like Mary, but she couldn't be. Mary didn't walk like that. Mary kind of shuffled along.

But this person with the same bronzy-reddish hair bounced along like a ten-year-old girl. She was coming closer and still looked like Mary! She raised her arm with a silly big wave above her head. She gave a wave of "Hey! Here I am! Hello!" and a big smile beamed across her face.

It was Mary!

Joanna and Mary ran toward each other, and locked in an embrace and wept with joyful emotion.

"You're alright?" Joanna sobbed.

"Never been better!" Mary laughed joyfully.

Joanna was speechless. The air was charged with emotion, yet there was nothing to say, so she simply grabbed Mary again, relieved to have her friend back in one piece.

For the next couple of hours, Joanna listened to Mary's stories of Jesus. In the days following her deliverance, Mary had followed Jesus from Capernaum to several other fishing villages along the coast. She detailed every miracle she had seen. Joanna listened politely, and then excused herself, and proceeded to head home.

Joanna was alone for the walk back home, or so she thought until Crabolus appeared out of nowhere.

"Pssst," he whispered from behind a tree.

Joanna jumped, "Crabolus! You scared me!"

Crabolus had the same scowl as the time he accused her of giving a bad report to Herod.

"You remember our little secret?" Crabolus hissed, grabbing her by the arm.

"Of course," Joanna trembled.

"I am told you do not approve of my two friends."

"Two friends?"

Crabolus twisted her arm until it hurt, "Yes, friends. Ephraim and Namen. If you do not help them and do as they say, it will not go well for you. You understand I have been promoted to guard at the palace. I have ways of guarding, that you have not yet seen!"

Joanna struggled to get free, but Crabolus was much too strong. "I will..."

Crabolus twisted the arm further, until Joanna collapsed to the ground. "I will... what, Joanna?"

"I will help them," she made out.

"Now that's better!" Crabolus sneered, "Ephraim and Namen may not be here to watch what you do, but I am! If I hear another word of you complaining against the Parthians, I will have a little talk with Chuza, and you know what that means!

"Oh, my! You could be stoned for that!" With that he disappeared down the path.

Joanna brushed the dirt from her knees, and wiped her eyes. What more could go wrong! What do I do now?

Chapter Twenty

Herod's Terrible Birthday Party

Despite Crabolus' attempts to get other people to do his dirty work, the two parties at the palace were moving ahead. All the servants and attendees of the court were busy making the detailed preparations. Herod was ruler over Galilee, and what better way to show off his pompous kingship than to throw a birthday party for himself!

Therefore over the next number of days, he commanded the best of food, décor, and presentations to be offered.

And when the great day of celebration arrived, Herod came out in fantastic attire. He had decked himself in ornamental chains of gold, and flaunted a new scepter never before seen.

Now that people from all over the country had arrived, the party was set to begin. The most famous of them were seated at exquisitely decorated tables. By Herod's request, these tables were strategically placed, close to the king, in order to be in earshot of his self-exalting comments.

Herod announced the first presenter of the night, the court jester. The jester appeared, in a costume easily recognized by all. He adjusted his hat, long and loose gloves, and water-stained boots.

"I have come to display my amazing talent," he mocked, "as a Galilean fisherman!" The crowd cheered. Everyone knew the coasts of Galilee flourished with simple-minded fishermen. Romans despised them, since most of them had little education. They even spoke with a unique accent, recognized and judged by those in prominence.

The jester proceeded to present a mime. He had brought a fisherman's net for a prop, and pretended to be grabbing his fish out of the net. The projected problem, found to be quite amusing to the guests, was the poor fisherman couldn't get his hand securely on any of his 'fish'. His imaginary fish slipped onto the floor. The jester jumped back to illustrate a fish flopping back toward him. At one point he chased imaginary fish across the floor to the feet of Herod's closest guests, even onto their legs. The crowd crowed in laughter.

Next, the jester had two servants bring a real fisherman's boat into the court. He jumped in, and began to 'row'. He sang a well-known Galilean fisherman's song as he rowed his boat. All the guests smiled at the familiarity of the song. The jester stood, and raised his hands, palms outward. He then jumped out of the boat, and across the court. Quickly changing his costume, he now became a "tax collector". His new costume brought a fresh wave of laughter to the audience. He now pretended to swim, and motioned to an imaginary fisherman in the boat to help him get to the side of the boat. Upon reaching his 'destination', the jester reached into his costume and presented a sign, which read, "Give taxes now!"

Herod roared in laughter with the crowd. "When you can't corner a fisherman for taxes, you have to go after him!"

Once the jester had finished, the guests continued to chat with each other. The servants came in with several delicacies, fruit, nuts, and other appetizers. Many of the prestigious ladies commented on who had attended and those who were missing.

Conspicuously absent was Herodias, his wife. Some said she refused to attend. The party was not about her, nor did she want to support the exaltation of her husband Herod. He had not thrown a party on her birthday. She was annoyed, especially after she saw his immense wealth being wasted on his own birthday!

But from Herod's standpoint, things made total sense. Being that it was a family affair, what better way to celebrate than to ask the very precious daughter of Herodias, Salomis by name, to dance before the crowd. Herod was sure his wife would hear of such extravagances, and it would enrage her all the more.

Salomis had pleased the crowds a number of times before, and now that she was at the marrying age, her beauty and gracefulness was fully formed. She danced with elegance unmatched by anyone else.

The music intensified, and she twirled into the center court. She presented a mix of traditional Roman moves, augmented with bolder, more erotic moves. These she had carefully learned by watching women from Egypt, Asia, and beyond, who had immigrated to Galilee.

The crowd loved it!

Herod was ecstatic! He turned to Salomis grinning and nodding vigorously, "What an amazing talent you have!"

The crowd cheered once again, waving white handkerchiefs, and towels. Herod smiled, knowing he had pulled off another Roman masterpiece.

Now his softer side needed to show off, and he would show his generosity—a gift of sorts for himself! The moment the dance ended, he called Salomis to his side, and stood up to address the crowd.

"Give praise to this young lady! She is an amazing dancer!"

The crowd agreed, and called back, "Praise you, King Herod, our ruler and royal potentate! And praise to your daughter, the lovely Salomis!"

Herod held up his hand to quiet the crowd, "I declare that I will give to Salomis anything she so desires, up to half of the kingdom!"

Salomis flushed at the acknowledgement. One could barely hear her response, but she quickly left the palace floor.

"She's gone to ask her mother," the crowd whispered to one another excitedly. "She won't be long. She will not want to keep the king waiting."

When Salomis returned, the lines of her face were taut, and she couldn't speak.

Salomis looked at Herod, at the crowd, and then again at Herod. "I cannot bear to say it!"

Herod assured her loudly before the entire audience, "Speak it out! I am not a poor man who cannot follow that which he has promised. Do not hold back—Ask what you will!"

Salomis swallowed, and seeing her mother now in the doorway of the auditorium, affirmed her request: "I... we request of the king, the head of John the Baptist, here and now, on a plate!"

Herod stuttered. He had promised, and had expected a request of money. Putting John in prison was hardly justified, and he had so commanded during a fit of rage. But truth be known, he admired the man, and wanted to keep him close in order to hear him again. Now he risked looking like a fool in front of the nobles, chief leaders of the land, and also his own family. He dare not refuse her request. It was John's head, or his reputation.

Herod's squinty eyes blinked at an invisible spot on the floor near his nervous foot which shuffled from side to side. Finally he looked up. He stared for a moment at Salomis, and then glanced across the floor at the heinous smile on Herodius' face. He then scanned the crowd defiantly from one side to the other.

He shouted, "I am the king. Do as the girl has requested! Bring to me, here and now, on a plate, the head of John the Baptist!" Among the soldiers in attendance, one wore the black robe. He held a long, wide sword unsheathed. To this one Herod pointed, and then swung his pointed finger toward the gate leading out to the prison, and the executioner followed his command.

The crowd gasped!

Mark 6:17 For Herod himself had sent and laid hold of John, and bound him in prison for the sake of Herodias, his brother Philip's wife; for he had married her. 18 For John had said to Herod, "It is not lawful for you to have your brother's wife." 19 Therefore Herodias held it against him and wanted to kill him, but she could not; 20 for Herod feared John, knowing that he was a just and holy man, and he protected him. And when he heard him, he did many things, and heard him gladly. 21 Then an opportune day came when Herod on his birthday gave a feast for his nobles, the high officers, and the chief men of Galilee. 22 And when Herodias' daughter herself came in and danced, and pleased Herod and those who sat with him, the king said to the girl, "Ask me whatever you want, and I will give it to you." 23 He also swore to her, "Whatever you ask me, I will give you, up to half of my kingdom." 24 So she went out and said to her mother, "What shall I ask?" And she said, "The head of John the Baptist!" 25 Immediately she came in with haste to the king and asked, saying, "I want you to give me at once the head of John the Baptist on a platter." 26 And the king was exceedingly sorry; yet, because of the oaths and because of those who sat with him, he did not want to refuse her. 27 Immediately the king sent an executioner and commanded his head to be brought. And he went and beheaded him in prison, 28 brought his head on a platter, and gave it to the girl; and the girl gave it to her mother. 29 When his disciples heard of it, they came and took away his corpse and laid it in a tomb.

Chapter Twenty-one

The Invasion Begins

Two weeks later, Joanna returned to visit Mary's home in Magdala. As usual, they talked for hours.

Because of Joanna's curiosity, she decided to test Mary and what better way than to ask her about the two Parthian men. "So, how are Ephraim and Namen doing?" she said half-timidly.

Mary sat up straight, and looking Joanna in the eye, said matter-of-factly, "For one they haven't been around. For two, I am no longer interested in men that way. They're a part of my past."

"Not like you at all, Mary!" Joanna teased.

Still as serious as before, Mary replied, "I just don't think I'm ever going back to the way I used to be, Joanna."

"Hmmnn," Joanna made out, a little embarrassed at her own inquiry, "I hope you still like to have fun."

"I had fun with you in Capernaum!"

Joanna laughed, "I would call that more eventful than fun. I admit I had a little fun watching the Pharisees, and how Jesus can win any debate with them in seconds." She leaned over the table and now it was her turn to get serious, "So is everything alright now? I mean, you were really not yourself back in Tiberias. I was afraid you were going to do something awful to yourself!"

"That wasn't me, for true! I could tell you how it all happened. Do you want to know?"

"I'm not sure I do..." Joanna hesitated.

"I got involved in something evil a year ago. I spent some time with this man who, I discovered, was a witch. I didn't think evil spirits were real, but I found out the hard way. I let him put a spell on me. He said it would make me rich.

"The spell didn't make me rich. Right after the spell, crazy things started happening; noises in my house, noises in my head, and fear attacking me like... like—well you saw me."

Joanna nodded.

"What I didn't tell you is that these devilish attacks happened before... as many as ten times. I had started to fear for my life."

"So I wasn't wrong in thinking you could harm yourself!"

"Not at all," Mary agreed, "and I'm sure the witch put evil on me. That's when it all started."

"Oh," was all Joanna could say.

A strange silence ensued, lasting several minutes. During that silence, Joanna didn't only think about Mary's deliverance. After her encounter with Crabolus, she feared for her life. Crabolus just might be crazy enough to... she dared not imagine what he would do. But that conversation would have to wait. Mary may have discovered the powers of Jesus, but Joanna decided she wouldn't be the one to bring Mary into another crisis. She thought, Who knows what might happen to Mary, she just might revert into another breakdown.

Finally Mary laughed, "Joanna, we used to talk by the hour about men. And now what are we talking about? ... Jesus and spirits!"

Joanna managed a chuckle with Mary, "Yes, I suppose we've changed the topics of our conversation. I'm still not convinced about that prophet Jesus though."

- - -

The yellow sun of early morning had barely peeked over the horizon when Joanna woke up with a start. The sound of thunder was in the distance. Or so she first thought. She peered out her bedroom window, trying to figure out what was going on.

She stared into the sunlight. A massive cloud of dust rose up in the distance. Then she heard what had awakened her. The rumbling sound of an army vibrated the windows. They marched in from the north. A steady thrum, thrum, thrum accompanied the sound of boots on earth, and the noise sent chills up Joanna's spine.

The Parthians!

"Mary, get up!" Joanna exclaimed in a whispered rasp, "They're coming!"

Mary scrambled out of bed, and together they watched out their window. Two massive groups of horsemen flanked the sides, and thousands of military footmen marched up the middle. A full hour later, the entire army had passed by Magdala. The Parthian troops turned westward, and headed up the Valley of the Doves. They wound their way around the first bend, and disappeared from view. She wondered why they headed up the steep incline to Mount Arbel and the plateau to the west.

"They'll be camping somewhere up the valley, where they can find protection at night."

Joanna's face turned white with fear. "Do you think they'll attack in the morning?" Now her fear was the very catalyst that brought her to an unwavering decision. *I'll risk it all for Chuza and my friends at the palace. No matter what Crabolus does or says! No matter what Ephraim, Namen or Matus may do!*

"We've got to warn the palace!" she said to Mary. She was already wrapping herself in her outer cloak, and putting on her sandals. "Are you coming?" she asked a bewildered Mary, still trying to wake up.

"I… I need to stay," Mary stuttered.

"I'm going!" Joanna declared and, with that, headed out the door. She understood the dangers of traveling alone through the hills of Galilee. They already had had one encounter with rebels along the road between Magdala and Tiberias, but she would take the risk. Chuza was in danger, and she had to tell him. She might not be able to run as fast as Mary, but she was sure to be a close second.

The Parthian army had chosen to march west of Magdala, and Joanna figured she could pass undetected if she took the road south along the sea, and then over to the palace. One hour and ten minutes later, she rushed through the entrance of Herod's court, barely waving to the guards stationed next to the gate. She burst into the main entrance of Herod's palace and demanded, "Where's Chuza?"

The first attendant pointed down the corridor to the room most often used by Chuza in recording taxation and revenue. Joanna didn't wait for the usual protocol of kneeling and asking permission, but spoke breathlessly, "Chuza! They're coming!"

Chuza was alarmed by the terror on her face. "Who's coming? Tell me!"

"Parthians," she said with a raspy voice. "There nearly here!"

Chuza downplayed Joanna's intensity for the moment. "Yes, don't worry. Delegations from Syria, along with a few representatives from the Parthian empire, are meeting with Herod tomorrow morning. They have come in peace to negotiate trade between Galilee and the northern empires. There may be a group of five or six at the most and perhaps a few attendants with them. How many did you see?"

"About thirty thousand foot soldiers and horsemen!" she exclaimed.

Chuza's mouth dropped. Horror filled his face. Without a reply, he rushed out the doorway and down the hall to Herod's personal quarters. Proper protocol would seldom allow her to be present there, so she waited nervously by Chuza's recording desk.

She paced as she waited. Telling Chuza had to be the right thing to do, or was it? Here she was in Tiberias and Mary was in Magdala. The question now occurred to her why Mary wanted to stay behind. Perhaps, at this moment, Mary might be warning the Parthians that she still held allegiance to Herod, and had come to Tiberias to warn them? The thought of Mary off with the Parthians crushed her. Might it be true? There was no way of really knowing. But she doubted it. Mary's demeanor seemed changed, and she seemed more gentle than before.

Inside Herod's chambers, Chuza relayed the message to Herod. The facts were clear. An army was coming, numbering in the thousands.

"But we have only five hundred foot soldiers here!" Herod cried fearfully, "and it will take a week or more to get the Roman troops from Jerusalem here!"

Chuza reminded himself of another problem. He didn't trust anyone anymore. In addition to the breaches in the outer wall, some of the guards had reported the appearance of several strangers hanging around the palace. A number of them had been confronted and told to leave Tiberias, but their motives were never determined.

Herod called his advisors together, and deliberated about their options. His advisors suggested an attack would not be likely during the night hours. Even Parthian soldiers wouldn't risk their lives in the dark of night when structured ranking easily turned into utter confusion. Many enemy armies had found out the hard way. When civilians heard the battle in array, they often joined in the fight against them, causing great confusion for the invading troops. The civilians knew every nook and cranny on the landscape. They knew about tunnels, and caves, and hideouts used in several "attack and run" ventures. While civilians quietly groaned over the heavy taxation of Rome, when push came to shove, most refused to take up arms against Rome. A few had done so to their demise, and every Galilean heard the results.

Herod decided to wait until morning, and meanwhile, no guests were allowed in the palace.

Herod's voice trumpeted loud and clear. He pointed to a soldier in command, "You! Soldier there! Lexus! I want twenty guards covering all the outer gates!"

He looked over to yet another, "And you! You send some trusted men to check every room on the inside. They are all to be locked and stay locked! Take the rest of your brigade to stand vigil outside my personal quarters. Do you understand?

"And no delegates from Parthia or Syria tomorrow. If they come, send them back where they came from!"

Joanna watched the soldiers running back and forth through the corridors of the palace. Herod had indeed believed her report!

Chuza returned shortly after, with a rather startling announcement.

"You won't be going home tonight," he stated. "It's too dangerous. Everyone must stay at the palace. A guest room is being prepared for us, and should be ready within the hour."

Joanna was sure some of the guards had made agreements with the Syrian and Parthian cause. She hoped they had not been selected to keep gates secure during the night watch.

"Wouldn't we be safer at home?"

"These are the rules of Herod, my dear. And no, you would not be safer at home."

Joanna didn't like the mandate. But rules are rules, and she resigned to the fact that she would be sleeping at the palace for the night.

She thought of another issue which had far greater implications. She had divulged a lot of information to the Parthians. They now knew where Chuza kept the keys. They knew how to use them. Perhaps this was the night they would use them! They had a reasonable count of how many guards were at the palace. They had a list of the guards who were ready to overthrow Herod. Though they didn't know where each one was posted, Joanna was sure they would be contacting her at any time to find out.

She had betrayed Herod and her own husband, Chuza. Now all their lives were in danger because of her mischief.

Joanna tried to formulate a plan that would undo that mischief. But it wasn't that easy. For every idea she came up with, she had four reasons to not do it. Most of those reasons centered on the threats made against her by the Parthians, and their cohorts.

She made a mental list of all the guards and soldiers she could think of. For the next hour, she wrote down, on a small parchment, the names Matus had given her long ago.

Albus was first on the list. He was a guard with special duties in finance. He would often assist Chuza in counting the money. Certainly he knew the location of keys and such. And as Matus had said, at least three of them had gained trust with Herod himself.

Gnaeus usually was posted at the front gate. Joanna knew him well, and had often flirted with him as she entered and left the palace. Now the thought of him disgusted her. How convenient—a traitor at the front gate!

Joanna recalled the names of each guard, and a particular soldier, Cicero came to mind. Yes, Matus had definitely mentioned Cicero in his list. She didn't know much about him, other than he usually worked with Clapmore, a psychological misfit, who flitted about much like Crabolus.

Crabolus! How could she forget him! Not only was he an idiot, but a traitor!

She took her pen and wrote the other two names as she recalled them: Blasius, and Domitianus. She didn't know much about either one, but wondered if they were perhaps night guards.

Other names she couldn't recall. Once Herod uncovered these men, any other traitors shouldn't be hard to find out.

But telling Herod was the real problem. How could she warn Herod without admitting her own guilt? The first thing Herod would ask is how she got such information. Being questioned by Herod wasn't a road she wanted to travel, for sure. Perhaps if she left the list for the soldier in command, Lexus, in a place where only he would find it... No leaving notes laying around would not work either. She folded the parchment and tucked it up the sleeve of her dress, and headed down the hall.

At that moment, a runner called through the court gate with more news. Several more towns had been taken, all closer to Tiberias than ever.

Meanwhile, Herod sent runners to Jerusalem requesting help from their larger military ranks, but no one would expect them to arrive for many days.

The soldiers scurrying about made Joanna dizzy, so she made her way to the temporary sleeping quarters for her and Chuza. She entered the room, lit the lamp, and prepared to go to bed. Chuza wasn't there, but she didn't expect him any time soon, since he was likely with Herod.

A knock on the door was followed by a cheerful voice on the other side. "Joanna? Are you in there?" Miriam and Chaya had come with a plate of food. Both of them smiled from ear to ear, and Joanna knew their friendship had developed well. Most servants wouldn't go out of their way to help staff, but Miriam and Chaya were simply reciprocating Joanna's generosity and friendliness.

"We know it's not much, but here..." They presented Joanna with her favorite dish; veal with lentils.

"You are so wonderful! How did you know I would be here?"

"We recently saw Chuza, and he told us."

"You took him food, too? So nice! How kind of you to look after us like that."

Miriam and Chaya smiled again. Not many at the palace took time to appreciate the hard work of the servants. Most simply expected to be served, and complained when things went wrong. Joanna, on the other hand, had always stopped to chat with them, and even given them gifts on occasion. The two servants grinned with admiration at Joanna, and asked if she needed anything else.

"No, I'll be fine. We can only hope the palace will be safe!"

"Of course!" They nodded sincerely, and left the room.

Moments later, two soldiers arrived with a sampling of her wardrobe from home. The clothing included sleepwear for the night, and something fresh to wear for the next few days. Obviously the palace was preparing for a major lockdown, which might last for days or weeks.

At least they know how to look after a person, Joanna reminded herself. It also reminded her that in many ways, she was treated like a queen already, something the Parthians had shallowly promised her if she would only defect to them.

She reached into her sleeve to pull out the note and... It was gone!

There was no sleep to be had. Where was the note? She checked her other sleeve, every part of her garment in case it had moved up her sleeve. She checked the floor, her shoes, down the hall where she had walked, and couldn't find a trace of it. The note had unexplainably vanished!

Two hours later, Chuza showed up.

He took her hand, his voice shaky with concern. "I think we're safe for tonight," he said, "Herod has guards and soldiers posted everywhere."

Joanna suddenly had a thought about the keys, and decided to risk asking Chuza the question. "What about the keys?"

"The keys?" he repeated.

"Did you move the keys to another place? What if someone from inside the palace decides to turn against us?"

Chuza looked at Joanna in amazement. "You're absolutely right Joanna! Why didn't I think of that! We can't be too careful about this." He had already re-latched his shoes, and turned toward the door. "I'm going to suggest to Herod we move all the keys to a new location." He smiled at Joanna, and quickly disappeared to tell Herod.

Moments later he returned. "Herod had the keys moved and they are guarded by two of his best soldiers."

"Which soldiers?" Joanna asked, trying not to show her concern.

"Gnaeus and Blasius. Why?"

Joanna swallowed, turning white as a sheet. "I don't know," was all she could muster.

Chuza apparently didn't notice Joanna's reaction. He let out an exhausted sigh, and crawled into bed, more than happy to get to sleep. But for Joanna, sleep would not come. She moved her feet back and forth on the bed, and rolled from side to side. She snuggled close to Chuza, hoping he didn't notice she was still awake.

Adventure was one thing, but this was pure danger. If the Parthians were successful in their invasion, Chuza's life would be in danger, and hers too. Joanna felt her heart pounding as she fearfully thought about what might take place.

She thought, What can I do? I would like to run away and hide somewhere, but I'm not allowed to leave the palace! Oh, if only Mary was here now! She stopped a slight sniffle, and a tear rolled down her cheek.

I know what Mary would say: "You have to trust in God, Joanna." She almost blurted out, But I don't know how to trust Him!

Joanna lay motionless for a good hour. The passing hour became pure torture. Deep within, she explored every question of right and wrong. Over and over, she remembered each immoral encounter in detail, and wondered if she could ever escape her haunting memories. She honestly believed she was a good person, but the display of evil actions told quite a different story. She wrestled with broken trust, and the fear of getting caught in her sin. All she had ever known was deception, living an undercover life. The fear she now experienced was deeper than what the Parthians had caused. It was the very groan of a dying heart within her. At the end of an hour, she knew what she needed to do.

Joanna silently slipped off the edge of the bed, and knelt at a chair across the room.

She began to whisper, "God, if you can hear me, please help me now. I can't live this way anymore. I need your peace."

For the next two hours Joanna poured her heart out to a God she had never known before. At times she began to sob, and tears flowed down her beautiful face as though they were stored up, just waiting for such a moment. She vented no shrieks of deliverance, no loud calls for help. But in the quiet whispers, Joanna felt the powerful touch of God's Spirit, bringing the peace she had asked for.

Now she remembered something about God she had been taught as a child: "He is near those who are of a contrite heart." The moment she acknowledged the verse, she realized a tremendous change taking place within. "Yes!" she whispered, lifting her head, "You have heard my contrite heart, Oh God!"

Joanna looked over at the bed. Chuza had not woken up. Silently she walked over to the side of the bed. She slipped back onto her side of the bed, and fell asleep instantly.

Chapter Twenty-two

Conflict on the Horizon

Joanna was making her way across the courtyard about mid-morning, when two soldiers came rushing into Tiberias on horseback, dust being kicked up from their hoofs. They galloped around to the front of the gate, and screeched to a stop, their front hoofs skidding into the soft dirt. The horsemen slid off and gave the details. "Sogane has been taken by the Parthians," they announced, as Lexus opened the gate. "The city has been totally destroyed. They've broken down the gates, raped the women, and killed all the men and children in the vicinity. It's an awful catastrophe!

"They attacked Sogane from the north early yesterday morning. The city is in difficult terrain. We didn't expect Sogane to be vulnerable to the Parthians, but they came fast and strong in numbers. Now the Parthians are only a day's journey from Capernaum!"

"They were defeated because there are few Roman soldiers there. The town is an easy target," Lexus replied.

More news soon reached the palace. Everywhere Joanna went, people talked about the Parthians. The town of Genessaret had fallen to their advancements. Genessaret was now the closest city to fall prey to the Parthian advancement.

In the days that followed, the Roman army took their soldiers and sent them out. They hoped to prevent a full invasion of those areas, but it was too late. The Parthians had already fortified the towns, and struck fear into any opposition living in the country areas around Sogane and Genessaret.

Joanna regularly made her way to the gate of Herod's palace. The gate was often the place where current news was first given, and she wanted to stay informed. On this particular day, Lexus was again at the soldier's post, and recognized Joanna as she approached.

"How is the steward's wife?"

"Stuck here at the palace, just like everyone else," she replied.

"And Chuza?"

"Chuza is very busy with the steward's work."

Joanna knew it was merely small talk, but appreciated the fact that a high ranking soldier would even talk to her. She figured it had something to do with the respect Chuza maintained from everyone at the palace.

"Do you know what I would like to do?" Lexus asked.

"What?"

"I wish I commanded fifty thousand soldiers. I would go out, and just crush the Parthians!"

"That's a big dream, but I wish it were true," she looked ahead, "I hear we don't have many soldiers here." She thought of the implications for Lexus, and how things might turn out for all of them with so few soldiers at Tiberias.

"Well, now is the time for Rome to act, and though we might lose a few soldiers, we'll find a way to chase those lizards back to the east!" Lexus gritted his teeth as he talked. He spoke as though he imagined the battle taking place before his eyes.

Joanna tried to give him encouragement. "Yes, their defeat will be as it has been dozens of times before. The Parthians will go running back to their caves in hiding. Rome will once again secure its hold over the Galilean area and its people."

Half an hour later, the watchmen's horns sounded. Joanna watched as, within minutes, another group of soldiers appeared fully dressed. The centurion was decked with a semi-circular band attached to his helmet, protruding above his head. This distinguished him from the other soldiers, who had simple metal plates across their shoulder, chest and back. The centurion barked orders for his sections to fall into order, and within seconds they were perfectly in line. Eighty such soldiers of various ranks soon marched out through the gates. They then disappeared in a cloud of dust down the path toward the Sea of Galilee and on to Genessaret. Eighty soldiers wouldn't be enough to defeat the entire Parthian army, but they might be enough to deter them from attacking Tiberias.

Joanna had seen this pattern in the past, but she understood things that had escaped even Herod. The Parthians were ready, poised, and organized like never before. They had gained more support than ever from the common people, taxation being their greatest tool of argument.

Her observations were equal to reality, because two days later, it was not the Parthians running for cover, but the Roman soldiers who were soundly whipped by Parthian attacks. They crept back to Tiberias, carrying their wounded, and mourning their dead comrades. Joanna easily counted some of the recent towns taken by Parthia: Aphek on the east of Galilee, Chorazin to the north, and now Sogane and Genessaret.

Everyone from soldiers to servants felt the pangs of defeat. A week ago, the general populace hadn't been in a panic. Now, the morale had come crumbling to a terrible low when the next news arrived. Parthia had also taken Magdala, a mere twenty-four furlongs up the coast, and the home of Mary. As Joanna listened to the report, her throat became dry, her bones ached, and her whole body felt dreadful. People stood anxiously in the streets, chatting with their neighbors, not knowing what to do. Some gathered a few of their belongings, and fled to Sepphoris, a city staunchly Roman, who would never tolerate any foreigner in their midst.

Those who had previously served in the Roman army volunteered once again, and were enlisted. And the palace was again under a partial lockdown with no common people allowed to go in or out.

- - -

Later in the day Joanna was allowed to return home for a few hours. However, she was surprised when a man stopped her on the street.

"Matus!" she exclaimed in a whisper, "What are you doing here?"

Joanna felt her legs turning to rubber, and she tried not to show the shaking in her knees. Her heart beat rapidly.

Joanna

She had almost forgotten. Matus had told her someone would be giving her a message.

"I have a message for you," he stated coldly.

"A message?"

"Yes, I have come to give you the message myself. My other messengers have been busy stopping the runners of Herod on their way to Jerusalem."

"The runners didn't get to Jerusalem?" she said, now horrified at the thought.

"So now is the time for freedom. Soon the land will rest, and you will be like a queen."

"Uh, yes. I suppose you need my help in some…"

"This is what we need," he interrupted. "Next week you need to watch for some freedom fighters dressed in Roman uniform, standing outside the gates. We may need you to escort them into the palace.

"This is the most important thing; we need you to convince your husband Chuza to come and present the keys to help us open gates and doors. You will know what to do when the message comes to your home."

With that Matus disappeared down a path, and Joanna hurried home.

Joanna didn't understand. She had felt so free and peaceful within when she cried out to God in her room at the palace. Was the contentment going to be lost under this dreadful cloud of fear and panic? If the Parthians successfully invaded the palace, many would perish. Most certainly, Chuza and her would be either killed or taken as prisoners.

Suddenly she remembered something Jesus had said. Fear not, I am with You. You can ask anything in My name and it will be done. She fell to her knees in the middle of her room, and cried out, "Oh my God! Spare us from death! Spare us from the Parthian conquest!"

She lay on the floor, groaning in prayer for nearly an hour. Then in a moment, a simple vision formed in her mind. In the vision, she saw Parthians on horses stumbling, and fleeing, crushing their own soldiers as they fled.

She opened her eyes. What had she seen? A picture from heaven, she believed. But what could the vision mean? How could it even be possible for the Parthians to be defeated? They outnumbered the Romans greatly, and all Galilee supported them. I wish I could tell Chuza, she groaned inwardly, and I'd see what his reaction is. But I can't!

- - -

To everyone's surprise, the Parthians didn't invade Tiberias the next day, nor the next, nor the day after that. The Roman soldiers hoped reinforcements would soon arrive from Jerusalem, but as each day went by, there was no sign of them. Their only hope came at the expense of surrounding villages. Even though the Parthian army continued to camp near Tiberias each night, their missions seemed to target particular Galilean villages, but not yet Tiberias. The villages fell, one by one, and the Roman army had no power to stop them. Everyone was sure Tiberias was next.

Herod once again lifted the palace lockdown. This time, he allowed certain people like Chuza and Joanna to return to their homes for longer than just a few hours.

"Nice to be home again," Joanna sighed.

"No guests though. Not here, nor at the palace. Herod is strictly enforcing the rule."

"I'm too tired to have guests, anyway." She glanced over at Chuza. She discovered her heart was changing. She loved him in a new fresh way.

"You're a good man, Chuza." She smiled sweetly as he looked toward her, wondering where her remark had come from.

"Better than Herod?" Chuza joked.

"Much better than him."

"Speaking of Herod," she continued, "He doesn't seem to be quite the devil he usually is."

"Maybe you're right, but don't forget, you don't see him every day like I do."

Joanna longed to visit with Mary, but with the lockdown, Chuza refused to let her leave Tiberias. The Parthian army was too near, and Magdala now was under Parthian control. Chuza's refusal made sense. This time she had no problem heeding his demand. And Chuza seemed more loving in return, and had told her on several occasions how appreciative Herod was to have the keys more secure.

If only I could find a way to warn Herod about his enemies right here at the palace, she thought.

It was exactly a week since she had knelt down and prayed. Now she was living and sleeping at home. Before going to sleep, she now regularly prayed. Sometimes she sat on a chair, sometimes on the floor. Her favored position was to kneel by the chair. But on this particular night, she was in bed and so prayed a quiet prayer as she lay next to Chuza. Soon she fell into a deep sleep.

The night was overcast, and incredibly dark. Hours later, she was still sleeping deeply when, in the middle of the night, she was startled by something and awoke. She lay still, wondering what had awakened her, but there was no sound. She listened intently for a long time, but could only hear the drumming of her heart. She stretched her eyes open, but couldn't see so much as a shadow. She was wide awake. And as suddenly as she had awakened, a plan formulated in her mind. This time the message didn't come as a vision, but as a strategy in her mind, as clear as though it had been written on a scroll. Every detail of the plan was incredibly distinct, and she knew the plan came as a miracle from God.

She nudged Chuza next to her. "Chuza!" she whispered, "Listen to me!"

Chuza, startled, didn't know what to think. "What's going on?"

"I've got a plan!" she said excitedly. So she began to relay her plan to Chuza, who was still trying to wake up. But as soon as she revealed a few details, he immediately jumped out of bed and lit the lamp. He returned with pen and scroll in hand, listening carefully and writing down each point.

"Do you think it might work?" she looked him in the eye.

"Joanna, as crazy as this sounds," he exclaimed, "that could really work!"

"Even coming from me?" Joanna chuckled.

"I haven't forgotten about the keys, you know!"

Amazed, Joanna replied with a coy smile on her face, "And who would believe a plan like this? Coming from a woman that is!"

He instantly rushed off to find Herod.

Chapter Twenty-three

When Miracles Work

When Joanna woke up in the morning, Chuza had returned from the palace, and was fast asleep beside her. Joanna leaned on her elbow, and gently nudged Chuza.

"Chuza!" she whispered, to which he groaned, rolled over, and finally opened an eye.

"Chuza!" she repeated, "What did Herod say about the plan?"

"Herod thinks you are incredibly clever, and the most beautiful woman in the world!" he teased. He reached over and tussled Joanna's long hair with his index finger.

"Chuza! Tell me the truth! Really!"

"OK. You know Herod isn't going to broadcast that a woman has a great military plan. However, he doesn't mind taking ownership of somebody else's ideas, and projecting them as his own."

"I don't care," Joanna sat up excitedly, "just as long as it works!"

They made their way over to the table, and took a chair across from each other.

Chuza began to lay out Herod's plans, "Well, this is what Herod is going to do today. He believes that the Parthian army will eventually attack Tiberias, and doesn't trust the Roman reinforcements to make it on time to help. Thus the plan is to gather the soldiers today, and move them into position this afternoon. For three days, the Parthian army has moved into neighboring villages, capturing community after community. But Herod has noticed a developing pattern. Every night, they return to the seclusion of the Valley of the Doves, just west of Magdala. Because of the steep climb up at the further end of the valley, the Parthians haven't thought it necessary to place soldiers all the way up to the top of Mount Arbel. All they have for security is a few sentries in the narrowing path which leads westward up to Nazareth, and perhaps forty at the eastern end of the valley, where it spreads toward Magdala and the Sea of Galilee. So they are well protected on either end of this valley. A small army like ours couldn't possibly win a battle at either end of this gorge. However, no one is guarding the areas directly above their camp. They can't imagine anyone scaling the cliffs down to their camps with any success. No one could do that without being spotted. Archers couldn't possibly shoot their arrows with any accuracy from the top of the cliffs. But.... Who would think of the possibility of defeating thousands of soldiers by stoning them?"

"So he is going to use my plan, then?"

"Completely! This afternoon, while the Parthian army is out capturing who knows what village, Herod is going to set mechanical slings in place."

"They must be placed in such a way so they are not seen from below," Mary reminded him.

"Of course! Herod knows the capabilities of the 'kicking donkeys' as they are called. These rock-throwing slings will be set in place at the top of the cliff, overlooking the valley below. As you say, they will be placed just far enough back to be unobservable by the Parthians. Ammunition won't be a problem, because the top of the cliff is laden with rocks a good cubit in diameter."

Joanna measured her arm from elbow to hand. "Yes, a cubit-sized rock is good. Two cubits would be perfect."

"Now here's the thing Herod figured," Chuza continued, "the larger rocks won't carry as far, but it won't matter. We're not trying to break down a walled city here. We just want large, heavy rocks in order to create havoc for the Parthians below. All the slings need to do is send them over the cliff. Once the rocks are launched over the edge, they will roll down the cliffs and across the valley, just like you envisioned! I actually dislodged a rock once when I was a child at the very place. I had fun watching the rock go crashing down the cliff and across the valley floor!"

Chuza continued to fill her in on the Herod's details. "In addition, select soldiers will be lowered to caves below during the night, to await for the time of attack. Once all the rocks are launched, they will lower themselves the rest of the way down for hand-to-hand combat." Chuza grinned with the plan at hand. "The Parthians likely don't even know the caves exist. But every Galilean knows, and Herod's army does as well!

Joanna reviewed the plan in her mind. The exercise would create havoc at the very time the army was returning from their daily trudge through the heat. From the reports of observers, the Parthians always returned about an hour before sunset. They also kept meticulous formation until they reached their camp half-way up the gorge. The fact that they were so precise in rank would actually help the Romans to be successful. To make the plan work, they needed the Parthians to be close together, and needed the horses to be mounted and marching together. What the Parthians considered their strength would be their demise.

"The Parthians aren't so smart, staying in the same spot every night, are they? I guess it's because of their 'attack and retreat' method of warfare. It's what they do best, but we've found their weak spot. We're going to completely triumph over them, aren't we, Chuza!"

"You sound like a general, Joanna! Yes, they are ripe for destruction! With our military's skill and tactical advantage, we should be able to drive them out." Chuza looked her in the eye with admiration, "Good job, Joanna! This is going to work!"

They sat smiling across the table. It was a moment they had not shared in a long time. Perhaps their joy had been from another era, one where two young lovers had been incredibly attracted to each other. In a way, love was a miracle to recreate. Either way, it had been a long time coming. He reached out and took her hand, and clasped it lovingly in his. There they sat silently, not counting time; Joanna with a satisfied countenance, and Chuza, content and not hasty to run off to work.

Joanna's smile had turned to satisfaction, and she pursed her lips thoughtfully. After the silence, she was the first to speak, "Chuza, how does a person give allegiance to something they only support in part?"

Chuza put his hand to his chin, and stared down at the table for a moment, "I'm not sure what you are getting at…"

"Well, isn't it true on every level? We hold allegiance to Herod, yet hate his personality. We hold allegiance to the concept of national improvement and justice, yet hate excessive taxation. We hold allegiance to marriage, but we don't agree about everything. The people show allegiance to Rome, but inwardly, they love the ideals of the Parthians and Syrians. People have allegiance to God, but reject Jesus."

"Hmmn. Jesus. Now that's a deep subject. Sure funny how religion can mess up the world."

"Mary was pretty messed up before she found Jesus. She seems a whole lot better now."

"Well, I guess I'm glad for her.

"I'd like to meet him sometime," Chuza continued, "after all this trouble with the Parthians is over, that is." For just an instant, a mischievous smile appeared on his face, which Joanna didn't understand. But she was quick to respond to the idea of meeting Jesus.

"We'll both go!"

Chuza ignored her statement for the moment, and remained silent. His short smile had turned more thoughtful, and Joanna couldn't discern if he was thinking about Jesus, Parthia, or both. Either way, Joanna wasn't ready to push the point, nor was she ready to disclose her past connection to the Parthians. However, deep within, she felt the shift. Something was changing for the good. Maybe it had something to do with renewed feelings for Chuza. Maybe it had something to do with what she saw in Mary after her encounter with Jesus the Messiah. She couldn't quite put a finger on it, but sensed something significant had happened the night she knelt in prayer. It had been a defining moment. And wherever that defining moment would take her that would be the place she would go. And life would be good.

Chuza stroked his chin methodically, and then, leaning on his elbow, looked straight at his wife. "So what do you think?"

You're kidding! Joanna thought, realizing how unusual it was for Chuza to ask her what *she* was thinking. Now it felt like Chuza could see right through her. "What do *I* think?" she said.

She tried to speak without revealing her face that had begun to flush. "Uh, think about what?"

"About allegiance. How do we choose allegiances when, all around us, no one is perfect?"

"Oh, that!" she said embarrassingly, "We love each other, don't we?" She laughed. It had been a long time since she had used the word 'love' in her relationship with Chuza.

"Well, yes," he chuckled, "and do you suppose there are things about each other we hate?"

The question didn't need an answer, but Joanna reaffirmed in her own mind that things weren't as bad as she had made them out to be. Even though Chuza was often too busy and too removed from home life, there was no denying he was a loyal and caring husband. Men like Crabolus and Herod couldn't even begin to compare with him, in looks or pleasant respectability. Nor could any of the men with whom she had had affairs. She choked at the thought.

"I think we reach out with a caring hand, and overlook the faults of those we love," she stated matter-of-factly.

Chuza nodded. He smiled, knowing he was at least in part the recipient of her good will.

After a moment, he continued on the previous subject. "So what do you know about this Jesus man?"

"Jesus really changed Mary."

"In what way?" Chuza wanted to know.

"In every way. Mary was... well, you know... she really lived life in the danger zone..." Joanna struggled to describe Mary's activities without being too descriptive. After all, she had also been quite a flirt, but not to the extent of Mary. "Mary seems more settled and content. But I must say, she certainly has this new obsession for Jesus."

"Now you're telling me that instead of living the wild life, she lives with wild religion!" He raised his eyebrows, and looked at her for a response.

"Yes, you've got it. She even gave what little provisions she had, to Jesus and his disciples."

Chuza perked up with an even greater interest at the mention of money. "It has been said by one of our Jewish philosophers that 'the love of money is the root of all evil.'"

Joanna was startled, "What? Do you know who that Jewish philosopher is? I'm very surprised that you can quote it."

Chuza chuckled, "Of course I know! Mary isn't the only one who has an interest in this Jesus fellow! Alright, I admit; I stopped to hear him the other day."

Joanna's chin dropped. "You? You stopped to hear Jesus?"

Chuza grinned, "Yup! And guess what he was preaching about?"

"Money?"

"Like I had a target on my cloak, Joanna!"

"Mary says He knows everything about everybody!"

"You're starting to scare me," Chuza coughed, "Either this guy is a prophet, or he's a witch!"

"Mary says he's a prophet, for sure!"

"Mary says, Mary says!"

"But Chuza," Joanna retorted, "Giving money to the man who makes quotes about money can hardly be the vice of fools!"

"If fools could even think that deeply! No, I believe Mary's intentions are virtuous enough. It just baffles me that people are willing to give their money to Jesus after Caesar has already wrenched his quota from their pockets. I mean, how do they have anything left to give?"

Joanna recalled the genuine smile that Mary proudly wore when she was telling her about giving a sizeable gift to Jesus' disciples.

"People are always willing to give to a cause they believe in," Joanna stated to Chuza, rather obviously.

Chapter Twenty-four

Clapmore

Later that morning, Joanna left her home and walked over to the palace. As it happened, she arrived at the exact time the army was leaving. Lexus, now in a centurion's uniform, commanded his troops, with the specialized soldiers filing behind him. Slings had already been rolled out from their storage barns. Several of the soldiers began to pull and push them over the rocky terrain up the hill to the west.

The Roman strongmen, a good percentage of the entire small Roman army at Tiberias, made their way west of Tiberias, led by Lexus.

"Haaah!" Lexus yelled in time. At times the soldiers had to manually lift the slings over larger boulders. Soon Tiberias disappeared from the hills behind them. Now they were far from the security of the palace. Lexus scanned his troops, knowing the fate of Tiberias rested on him and his few soldiers.

As they continued to ascend upward, Lexus became silent. They were nearing their destination. The ascent was not as steep as before, and now they turned northward toward the plateau atop the Valley of the Doves.

Lexus noted the plateau extended flatly right to the edge of the valley's cliffs. They could not be seen from below. Also, just as earlier detected, not even one Parthian guarded the area. The spot was perfect for an ambush and was comfortable too. Numerous trees even sheltered them from the wind.

He led the Roman soldiers into the open area, and then abruptly stopped, raising his hand for the group behind him to do likewise. They stopped instantly. "Prepare the kicking donkeys!" he whispered to the men behind him, who spread the word back down through the ranks. The soldiers stealthily sprang into action, lining up the slings on one side, and erecting the tents near the trees on the other side. Lexus and the captains supervised the positioning of each rank of the soldiers.

Few words were spoken. Lexus used his arms to point. The sentries already knew what to do. They scouted out any areas along the cliff, where they could hide from any prying eyes below. Lexus pointed further along the plateau, and the watchmen padded away from the clearing. They would search for high places, with a good view in every direction. The watchmen would have to brave the cold breeze that moved down the mountain slopes. They would not make the same mistake of the Parthians. No security was good enough. This was a top secret mission, one which demanded their utmost attention, and right now it was to be silent. No fires. No talking. Just an eerie quietness as they moved about, like shadows in robotic symmetry.

Lexus motioned for the arms of war to be moved closer to the edge of the cliffs. They remembered that the Parthians would return from their daily operation just before dark.

Lexus thought about his brief conversation with Joanna. If only he had fifty thousand men! On the other hand, too much could go wrong with a massive army like that. He would make sure the best would be done with the few they had. Lexus would have liked to trumpet the call to battle immediately, but he knew the plan. Wait until the Parthians return. Wait until they were hungry and tired out. Wait.

Below them, in the shade and shelter of Mt. Arbel's cliffs, the few Parthians who serviced their camp stirred occasionally, preparing meals for the returning soldiers. The sentries could see the odd puff of campfire smoke wafting up and over the cliffs. The smell of boiling meat and vegetables carried right to the Roman camp, sending the aroma across the very place where they had hidden. But the Romans would not be distracted even when hungry.

However, during this set-up maneuver, Lexus noticed Clapmore, a second-ranked soldier close to the edge of the cliff. He almost wrecked the whole plan. While they pushed one of the slings closer to the cliff, Clapmore tripped over a sharp rock and almost fell head-first over the cliff. A nearby soldier lunged forward, grabbing Clapmore by the leg, and pulled him back from the edge of the precipice. Worst of all, he let out a sharp yelp of pain and sent stones scattering across the plateau, some falling over the edge.

Lexus immediately raised his hand, and all the soldiers froze, staring at Clapmore. Now Clapmore was securely hoisted up to level ground, and the centurion looked him over, head to foot to see the extent of his injuries. They were only scratches! Why the sharp yelp of pain, he had no idea, but shook his head in disgust. He then motioned with his hand for Clapmore to retreat to the far reaches of the sentries, where his actions would not be so risky.

"Klutz!" Lexus muttered at Clapmore as he shuffled past, his head bowed submissively. Lexus determined another mishap would not happen under his command. He once again went through a mental checklist, peering at the various levels of his troops. For a third time, he examined the slings, this time from a distance, ensuring they were armed and ready.

Lexus crossed his arms proudly as he remembered how the soldiers had strained to lock them in place with powerful tension. The slings were the most advanced weapon of offense. Four of his soldiers could prepare the tension arm within a minute. Rocks weighing enough to break through a walled city could be placed in its cradle and subsequently flung through the air towards the enemy. However, this mission held a vastly different purpose for the slings. Lexus was convinced they would be effective. The slings were not going to be aimed at a city, or the gate of a city. Instead, at the precise time, giant rocks, twice the usual size would be launched simultaneously. Lexus had eight 'kicking donkeys' lined up along the cliff. Each sling was close enough to ensure the giant rocks would make it over the cliff's edge. They just had to be sure the slings weren't too close. They didn't want to be spotted from below.

Lexus narrowed his eyes in the direction of Clapmore, wondering what had gotten into him. He didn't need anybody to jeopardize the entire mission. Even the best of soldiers might inadvertently trip over a rock, but the centurion wasn't so sure about this one. A man of experience, he kept his eyes open, inspecting the ranks. He reminded each soldier that any act of mischief would be treated as treason, and quickly dealt with.

They were ready. The sun still beamed high in the sky, and Lexus knew they had a long time to wait for the Parthians to return. From the outset of their arrival on the cliff tops, the sentries had been posted on both ends of their position, and a rear guard had also been set in place. The Roman contingency was in no way going to make the same mistake the Parthians had made.

The passing time seemed endless, but no one dared move or speak. The managers of every sling kept their eyes on the captain standing under a tree in the center of the operation. He in turn, kept his eyes peeled on the sentries who would be the first to hear or see the Parthians.

Hour by hour the sun slowly made its way across the sky. It was a long and boring wait, but Lexus knew he dare not become inattentive to the mission at hand. And the army knew that unless the Parthians changed their pattern, they would arrive back to their base camp about the same time as usual. The Roman's indication was the sun. When it became low in the sky but not yet behind the hills in the west, they would expect the army to return. But the sun was yet several hours from setting.

Chapter Twenty-five

Tiberias Under Siege

Back at the palace, the scouts returned at the usual time.

"The Parthian army has left their base in the valley, and are heading north," they announced to the soldiers guarding the palace gates.

Joanna tightened her jaw with concern as the scouts gave the monotonous details of how many, and at what hour they had observed them. She walked back home, relieved and assured the Parthians had at least headed the other direction.

Once she reached her home, she paced. She straightened a few things on the table. She looked out the window. She walked over to her bed, and sat down on its edge. She got up and looked out the window again.

Finally, she decided to return to the palace. Perhaps Chuza needed her help. There was no sense staying at home by herself.

She entered the palace gates, and then she heard a dreaded sound. The noise was only a muffled echo among the hills at first. But it was the same 'thrum, thrum, thrum' of marching boots she first heard at Mary's place. She instantly knew the sound.

The Parthians were coming to Tiberias! But how was it possible? They must have doubled back!

Two scouts galloped in through the gates within seconds. The announcement they had been dreading for weeks was now being trumpeted throughout Tiberias and the palace.

"They're coming!"

Herod appeared out of nowhere, "Shut the gate! Blow the horns!" Herod was beside himself. His face was red with fury and fear at the same time. He ran from guard to guard, grabbing them by the sleeves, and pushing them into place. He grasped the gate with his own arms, and pushed it with the help of the guard. The Parthians were rattling the very nerve center of his power.

Chuza and Joanna rushed back to the hallways of the palace, and Joanna took a number of servants with her into the protected room. She had slept in the same room only a week before. Even from there, she felt the ground shaking and heard the marching of the Parthian troops just outside Herod's palace.

Joanna gathered the humble servants around her, many whom were sobbing uncontrollably. Joanna mustered her determined thoughts. This is it! she thought, Now is the time for me to make a stand. I'm going to do it, for me, for Chuza, and for God! She motioned for the group to listen to her.

Several of the women stuttered, "What are we going to do? We have nowhere to escape!"

"We're going to pray!" she boldly announced to the trembling servants, "God will give us the victory!"

"Then we will pray with you!" said Miriam excitedly, and most of the others nodded their agreement.

Another of the servants stated, "I have met Jesus, and decided to be His disciple. I know He will do a miracle for us!"

Chaya broke in, nodding, "Yes! Do it Joanna. Let's pray!"

Joanna began to pray in earnest: "Oh great God Almighty. We believe that you are greater than this army who has come against us! Now help us, O Lord!" It seemed like a strange prayer and much too short, but it came from her heart.

Joanna was convinced her vision was from God, but now, she could hear the approach of the enemy. Prayer didn't come without fear, and it seemed harder to believe. But I do believe! she repeated the words over and over in her mind.

Like an approaching storm, the sound of marching feet got louder and louder. Dust billowed up from the roads as they stomped into Tiberias.

The gates to the palace had been firmly locked in place. People in the streets of Tiberias had fled, some to their homes, some to the hills.

Soon, the massive army stomped up and down every street in Tiberias. People huddled in their homes, hoping beyond hope that somehow they would be spared. The Parthian soldiers stood outside the gates of the palace yelling at the walls, throwing stones over the gates into the courtyard. The guards and servants within scrambled for cover.

The ground shook! So did the hearts of all the palace staff who shuddered in fear, gathering in small groups within.

Now the noise seemed to lessen. Joanna peeked out the door of her room and across the courtyard toward the main gate. All the guards had fled to inner rooms. All, that is, except three: Plouton, and two soldiers. He was trying to open the gates, but the locks that held them in place would not work with the keys he had. Without the locks disengaged, the gates would not budge!

Joanna heard a sharp command from the Parthian officer on the other side of the palace wall. At once, the enemy army turned and marched down the hill, chanting in triumphant celebration, and headed toward their evening resting place. They had observed the lack of Roman response, and assured themselves they would win tomorrow's battle.

On the inside of the wall, Joanna couldn't believe it! The Parthians were leaving! They must have decided it was too late in the day. The sun had been moving to the west, and shadows were indeed lengthening. But no doubt, they would return in the morning.

Everyone in Tiberias agreed that the huge show of Parthian force was the prelude to attack day. They sensed the Parthians meant to strike fear into the Romans, and that they accomplished in full measure!

Joanna returned to her attendants, who were still arm-in-arm in a circle of prayer. She announced to them that the Parthians had left, and they lifted their heads from prayer, and loudly yelled, "Hallelujah!"

This quickly brought Chuza to the room. "What's going on?" he asked, perplexed.

"We have prayed to our God! He will deliver us!"

Joanna grinned at Chuza, who still stood in the doorway, staring at the women of faith standing and smiling at him! He took a step toward Joanna, but didn't know what to say. She had obviously filled their room with a bunch of praying women! Chuza lifted his arm and turned his head at an angle.

"God, you say? Alright then... Let it be as you say. May God deliver us!"

Chapter Twenty-six

Trouble on the Hills

Lexus shuffled his feet nervously. The silence in the camp was endless. He had been trained to bark out his commands to the troops, not to do spy missions. He reminded himself of the importance of this mission, and his responsibility to Rome. His greatest command at the moment would not be to shout, but to trust every soldier to remain silent.

The last ray of the sun barely peeked over the hills to the west. Shadows became long and fuzzy in the mist of the evening. Was it possible they were one day too late, and Tiberias had been conquered? He dared not think of it.

At one point, he thought he had seen smoke ascending up from the east, near the area of Tiberias. He became unsettled at the sight. However, he soon realized it was simply some low clouds blowing in off the sea, and nothing more.

He looked back the other way, and noted the sun had now fully set behind the hills. The Parthians should have come back long ago. It seemed like an eternity had passed and the Parthians were nowhere in sight.

However, about half an hour later, the camp stirred suddenly.

The Parthians were on the way back to their home base!

The Roman sentries were barely visible, crouching behind rocks or shrubs near the cliff's edge. The air was filled with anxiety, but everyone stayed silent. Only the bulging muscles of their arms and legs indicated their readiness and nervousness for the precise moment to give the signal.

No one moved!

But Lexus couldn't believe his eyes when, at this most crucial time, the profile of a man appeared, walking in full view along the top of the cliff. One of the sentries sprang into action and jumped the man, dragging him back away from the cliff's edge. Lexus ran from his post to the scuffle. Two more soldiers helped pin the man to the ground.

Lexus stared down at the man. "Clapmore! What in Caesar's nation are you doing?"

"I left my spear!" he pleaded.

Lexus, unconvinced, ordered two of his soldiers to seize him.

"Take off his armor!" he whispered coarsely, sweat beading on his forehead. "Bind him, and guard him closely. He will not be causing any more havoc here!

"Don't let him out of your sight!" he added, spitting on the ground for emphasis.

Now that Clapmore was looked after, Lexus turned his attention back to the mission at hand. He hoped none of the Parthians below had seen Clapmore as he ambled across. He took a quick glance behind him. Though he had stationed sentries in several places, he just couldn't be sure... But they were all in place, and even a careful search indicated that no one else was out of rank. Even Clapmore was in his place; this time sitting cross-legged and bound, on the ground with two soldiers standing one on each side of him with their swords drawn.

He turned his head and scanned the scene before him. Eight mechanical slings, now armed and loaded with large irregular-shaped rocks, stood ready. He examined the sentries. They crouched on one knee with their right arm held slightly above their heads, high enough to be seen by the launchers, but not high enough to be seen below.

The silence was eerie. Tension mounted as every soldier fixed his eye on the upraised hands of the sentries.

Lexus slowly crept forward, and found a position next to one of the sentries. Now he could see the Parthians.

The thousands of Parthian soldiers, flanked by a hundred horsemen, slowly made their way up the dusty trail that led along the Valley of the Doves. The trail would lead them upward to the flat open area, where, normally, they set up camp every night. Lexus viewed the valley, which, at this point, was formed in a perfect u-shape. The cliffs fell off straight down, but then they rounded off at the bottom with a similar shape rising up the other side. Like a tub, Lexus logged it in his mind. Along the rounded parts of the 'tub', long grassy tufts grew up around the bare rocks, scattered here and there on the rolling slopes. It was the perfect layout for the mission at hand.

Lexus finally saw what everyone had been waiting for: Without so much as a sound, the sentry's arm thrust downward!

The horse riders didn't see what hit them. Gigantic rocks flew through the air, bouncing at high speed, and careening crazily down the sides of the valley. Seconds before they were struck, several horses along the outside row saw the rocks falling upon them. The horses tried to leap out of the way, their riders either hanging on for life, or being dismounted by the sudden rearing. The next row of horses, however, weren't so lucky. Giant rocks crashed into them at high speed, breaking their legs instantly. The domino affect was ugly. Horses trampled horses. Those horses first injured now caused major panic upon all the rest. Now all the horses jumped and stamped, and ran hysterically back through the entire rank of footmen, trampling hundreds. The surviving soldiers, in turn, were so shocked they simply turned and fled. Heaps of bodies lay on the ground where soldiers fell upon their comrades, most of them fatally wounded. The rest of the army scrambled their way down the valley, retreating hastily, a mad throng, fleeing crazily from the chaos that pursued them.

A mixture of screams and wildly neighing horses rang through the valley. Above them, the Romans raised their hands in victory, and yelled at the top of their voices. The fleeing Parthians below, hearing the cheering of the Roman soldiers, were decimated in heart, and, without any resolve to fight, simply ran for their lives.

It was later said by the common folk, that the entire Parthian army retreated with so much haste, they ran full speed into the sea of Galilee and so they all perished. In all likelihood, that was the embellished story etched in the minds of those who imagined such things. More truthfully, the entire army fled for their lives and were scattered throughout the plains of Judea.

Chapter Twenty-seven

Palace Cleanup

At Herod's palace, the Parthian spies grew restless. The keys they depended on did not work. No one had been able to unlock the gate, and now they were stranded inside the Roman complex. They were frustrated because no other Parthians would be joining them. The wait appeared to be too much for the Parthian spies within the palace. They decided to become heroes of their own.

Several of them gathered in a mob outside of Herod's quarters, and a few continued to try to find a way to release the palace gates.

Joanna and Chuza were startled when a servant banged on their door, looking for Chuza.

"Something is going on outside Herod's quarters. I think some guards are trying to break into Herod's room!"

Chuza bolted from the room with Joanna close behind him. About twenty guards and soldiers were posted in the courtyard. Several of them were now at the entrance to the hallway leading to Herod's quarters. The group recognized Chuza and Joanna, and began to clear the way for them to enter. But, before Chuza could move, Joanna looked behind her, and noticed something unusual about the men at the gate. Plouton appeared to be doing something with the gate, and the two soldiers with him looked out of place. Their uniforms had not been scuffed by combat, but brighter than the rest. Their boots were newer and more polished. They had not been used to the dusty winds of Galilee. At first, she thought the reinforcements from Jerusalem had arrived. But when she glanced in their direction, she saw them carefully observing her and Chuza, and for a moment their eyes met. She immediately knew who they were!

Joanna yanked on Chuza's arm, stopping him before he entered the corridor.

"The soldiers at the gate are imposters! I know it!"

Chuza gave her a blank response.

"Chuza! Those are the same two men who robbed Mary and I on the road to Magdala, and the same ones I saw in Rome. They dressed as soldiers in Rome too!"

Chuza would have dismissed what Joanna said, except for the fear written on her face. "Are you sure?" he asked.

"I've never been more sure in my life! Chuza, it's them! And Plouton got them their position!"

Chuza raised his eyebrows in surprise. He leaned closer to Joanna and whispered, "Alright, then. We need to be careful here. I don't know what's going on inside, but those men may be imposters as well."

Joanna quickly weighed the matter, and decided in an instant to divulge the information she had been withholding.

"Chuza!" she whispered back fearfully, "I can give you the names of the other traitors!"

To Joanna's surprise, Chuza reached into his side pocket, and pulled out a piece of leather with a list of names—the same list she had lost.

"It's your handwriting, isn't it?" Chuza looked her straight in the eye.

"Yes," she cried quietly, "and that's the list!" A tear rolled down her cheek as she stared helplessly at Chuza.

"I knew it! When I saw Crabolus on the list, I just knew it!"

"But Chuza! Some of them have keys! I'm sorry, Chuza. I should have told you but they wouldn't let..."

He took her by the arm, "Don't worry, Joanna. I'm looking after the keys!" He patted a pocket along the side of his cloak.

Chuza grabbed a prison guard by the arm and whispered, "Keep an eye on the two by the gate in the new uniforms. They are imposters, and if they try to follow us, thrust them through!"

The guard was startled by Chuza taking on the role of commander, but was too shocked to question him.

A group of supporters instantly formed around Chuza, ready to assist him in whatever way they could.

"Come on," he called, "let's find out what's going on."

They made their way down the corridor toward Herod's quarters. Already they could hear the ruckus at the end, near Herod's door. Fortunately, no one had been able to get the door open.

Several guards were trying to pry the door open, and when they spotted Chuza, they begged for his help.

"Herod is hurt!" they yelled, "but these keys don't work."

Chuza stopped to assess the situation. He knew why the keys didn't work, and was glad he had switched them all around earlier.

Joanna noted that the ones who wanted to gain entrance were on the list as well. Traitors! Liars! Herod was not needing help, but the imposters wanted help to get at him!

At that moment, a short man with black hair, and chiseled chin, appeared from the shadows, and reached out his hand to Chuza. "You must be Chuza! I am Neodius, soon to be married to the king's daughter."

Chuza took his hand briefly, then let go when Joanna let out a piercing scream behind him.

She screamed again, and this time she gained the attention of every person in the hallway and in front of Herod's room. "He's not Neodius!" she yelled, "He's an imposter. His name is Matus, and he's a Parthian spy!"

Joanna braced herself with her eyes fixed on Crabolus, Clemonts, Gnaeus, and all of the other heinous devils in this crime. She stood there, and in an instant she resolved what she had to do. Pointing her finger at the glaring crowd in front of her, she called out, "What seems to be is not. There is an underhanded conspiracy to overthrow Herod, and you, oh Crabolus are the one who is behind this all!" It was almost as though the hair on her neck stood on end as she spoke. One by one she pointed out the traitors. Those loyal to Herod took careful note, even though the chaotic crowd made it nearly impossible to apprehend any of them. The crowd was in confusion. Who was really who?

Chuza cared not that Joanna yelled at the crowd. Instead he quickly got the attention of a number of trusted soldiers, and let them know what was going on.

Joanna continued, her eyes now piercing Matus, "It is you! You are the one who sent a mob to Jerusalem, preventing Herod's messengers from getting there. You sabotaged the careful protection of my husband Chuza. You tried to seduce me to the Parthians, and sell myself to you, instead of being loyal to Caesar!"

Immediately, several of the traitors grabbed Chuza, and tried to wrench the keys from his control. "Down with Herod!" they yelled, "We want freedom!"

Joanna's voice screeched when they wrestled Chuza to the floor! "You are not for freedom, but for treason!"

She lunged across the hallway in the direction of Chuza, all the while yelling, "And I will have no part of such a mob as you are!"

She moved quicker than a cat. Matus tried to grab her, but she jumped up on a desk and reached for one of the lamps on the wall. It had worked against Herod once, but now it would work for him. She grabbed the lamp and tore it off the wall. She jumped off the table, shattering the lamp over the head of the Parthian who attacked Chuza. The oil contents splattered over the imposter and several others who tried to stop her, instantly igniting into flame!

Never before had anyone seen a woman so wild! She launched herself across the corridor to another lamp and repeated the procedure over a couple of other Parthians.

Chuza flung the door open, shrieking a whistle down the corridor. Within moments, servants scrambled from every corner of Herod's palace, declaring "stop the treason!" Soldiers armed themselves, and the mob was overpowered within moments, hands tied behind their back, feet tied with ropes, and the culprits were dragged to the dungeon.

Crabolus tried for an instant to draw his sword, but was overpowered by two guards. The other men, cowards as they were, simply surrendered.

Joanna still had a personal vendetta. She rushed back down the hallway, and gathered the attendants once again.

"Do you see that guard at the gate?" Joanna noticed that the other two had left, but Plouton still worked diligently on the gate.

"Plouton?" several of them asked.

"Yes. He is a traitor. Please believe me! And with your help I intend to capture him myself. You can see at this very moment, he is trying to find a way to open the gates so the Parthians can enter!"

"Oh," they gasped.

Joanna remembered how Plouton had so easily been drawn to the Parthians, and ready to betray Herod. She also remembered that Plouton had failed to pay her for her work just like the other Parthians. In fact, he had not paid her a shekel!

Joanna leaned over and spoke to the group huddled around her, "Miriam, I want you to take all the women and go hide around the corner over there. I will try to convince Plouton to come with me. When he rounds the corner, jump him and don't let him go!"

The women agreed instantly, excited to help.

"I'll get a rope from the stables!" Chaya volunteered, smiling, "...to tie him up with!"

"Let's do it!" Joanna said, and all the women scurried to their positions, out of sight.

Joanna waited for a short while, giving time for the women to post themselves. Plouton pried at some of the bars on the gate, and managed to bend some of them out of place. Apparently he had been so focused on getting the gates opened, that he had not heard the scuffles from the far end of the hallways. Neither had he seen the other traitors who were led away to the dungeons. Somehow in the midst of it all, he had kept his devious work intact, and undetected.

"Persistent pig!" Joanna sputtered as she started toward the gate.

She straightened her clothing, and dusted off the dirt from her battles along the hallway. Throwing her hair back, she moved closer to the gate and Plouton.

"Hello there!" she called.

"Joanna!" he said in relief, "Where can I find the key for these locks?"

"Plouton!" she smiled slyly, "Follow me." She beckoned with her hand, and led him across the courtyard, and he readily followed, expecting her to get the keys.

Joanna, leading the way, couldn't help but smile. It was a crowning moment. Perhaps it wouldn't mean much to anyone else, but it was the exclamation point on her decision to change her ways. She had put Chuza's life and reputation in danger so many times. This time, she would be the team mate that he deserved. She, with the attendants' help, would deliver Plouton in person to Chuza!

Her heart began to skip wildly as she rounded the corner. Like a wild animal led to a trap, Plouton marched expectantly behind her, until he saw the group of women gathered along the wall.

"What's this?" he questioned when Joanna turned around, and stopped right in front of him.

In the blink of an eye, Joanna grabbed his sword out of its sheath. Before he could move, the entire group of women was on him. They scratched and clawed him as he collapsed in a heap on the ground, holding his arms over his face to protect himself. They quickly grabbed his arms and feet, and tied them up with the ropes.

Then, grabbing an end of the rope bound to his feet, they mercilessly dragged him across the courtyard.

"Hey Chuza!" Joanna called out, "Look who we've captured!"

Chapter Twenty-eight

Things That Are Important

A few days after the Roman victory, Herod called both Chuza and Joanna to his quarters. Joanna couldn't help being a bit nervous about the meeting. However, when they arrived, Herod seemed unusually relaxed. He told them both to "sit" across from him at a small table. He appeared to simply want someone to listen to his ramblings about the victory over Parthia.

"The Roman army has re-gathered its forces. They have come from Jerusalem in the south and Iterea in the north. More are coming too. The Parthians who were hidden in caves and in homes of Galileans have all been flushed out.

"We have the best army, and always will! Hah! It only took them days to conquer them completely." Herod stroked his chin with pride. "No," Herod continued, "the Parthians will never master the skill, technology and power of the Roman army."

Herod nodded his head as he spoke, "And our citizens, Roman, Jewish... Yes, everyone is now showing their allegiance to Caesar." He growled as he added, "No one will ever defect to Parthia again."

Chuza wanted to assure Herod that all the money in the treasury was accounted for, so remarked, "We made it through without losing a shekel, Herod."

"Yes, I believe it. It is good!" he nodded again, without going so far as to extend thanks. But both Chuza and Joanna took his invitation to the meeting as the thanks they would get. They could tell he was relieved, and though he hadn't said as much, he appreciated their help.

Herod changed the subject, "Rome will reach to the farthest regions of Galilee. We will honor those who honor Caesar, and we will eliminate those who are against Caesar. Yes, I have decreed it. That is what we will do."

Joanna sat silently by, as Herod continued his post-battle report to them.

"Plouton... You flushed out that rat! Yesterday he was put to trial, and quickly disposed of. Yes, we found out he had falsified the approval of several imposters by using my seal. But no more! He is guilty of the crime, and now he is in the dungeons."

Joanna glanced at Herod for a moment. Herod was enjoying the moment, reminiscing the success of each power struggle. He was once again the ruler he had always been, a little dispossessed, and still a pawn in the hand of Caesar.

- - -

Two days later, a soldier arrived at the palace with a scroll in hand. It was for Joanna, from Mary. It read:

Dearest Joanna,

As you may know, the Romans have closed all the highways in Galilee. I am unable to come and visit, and therefore I thought you would like to receive my greeting, by way of a letter.

I do not know what may have happened to Ephraim and Namen. At any rate, it does not matter. I have a greater cause. I no longer want to give my attention to foreign militants. My devotion is solely for Jesus. I am convinced He is the Messiah, and once this military lockdown is lifted, I intend to find Him once again. There is no reason that I must stay in Magdala continually, so I will likely follow Him as He travels throughout the land.

I suppose I must find some work to do, and that I will find. For now, I am happy to have left the past, and will look forward to a better future.

I hope Rome will soon allow me the freedom to travel, and my first stop will be in Tiberias to visit you.

Your friend,

Mary Magdalene.

Joanna smiled. Mary was safe. She had been right in the center of the Parthians' attempted conquest, and survived.

- - -

Not long after, in the sunny morning hours, Chuza and Joanna reflected on what had happened.

"You're some woman, Joanna!" Chuza smiled.

"You know... It's not even about Rome or Parthia. It's about being loyal, and trustworthy with those you love. Whatever government is in charge on earth doesn't matter as long as your heart is governed by the Lord."

"You are completely right about that, Joanna."

A tear welled up, but Joanna just had to speak, "Chuza, I haven't been the wife you deserve. I've let you down terribly."

"Don't worry, Joanna," Chuza said softly. "I can see you are changing. I'm going to take more time for you too. I was so afraid of something happening to you the other night..."

"You mean in the corridor outside Herod's room?"

"I watched you. Seems to me you can defend yourself very well!" he chuckled.

"Maybe the Parthian attack woke up my senses. But I'll fight for you! You are more important to me than anyone else."

"It sounded to me that Jesus was the most important."

"Hmmn. Yes, and I'm still working on that one."

"I think I'm alright with that too. We should go hear Him out sometime — I mean you and I..."

"Yes, let's do that!"

Chuza and Joanna walked hand in hand slowly out to the middle garden. There, under a spreading olive tree, they embraced for what seemed to them like a blissful eternity. Still holding each other's arms, they turned to face each other, and Chuza said, "Joanna, I love you."

Silent for a few moments, Chuza finally continued with a wink. "You know, I could have sworn there was a time when I didn't trust you."

With that, he kissed her.

- - -

> Luke 8:1 Now it came to pass, afterward, that He went through every city and village, preaching and bringing the glad tidings of the kingdom of God. And the twelve were with Him, 2 and certain women who had been healed of evil spirits and infirmities — Mary called Magdalene, out of whom had come seven demons, 3 and Joanna the wife of Chuza, Herod's steward, and Susanna, and many others who provided for Him from their substance.

Author's Note

With some historical fiction now being taken as truth, I must clarify an important distinction. This is a story of "the way it might have been."

On the other hand, you will find quotations from the Bible throughout the novel, as it relates to Joanna and other characters. That is the true story, never to be changed by ages, or anyone's imagination.

Other than that, it is my hope that you were thrilled by the intrigue of Joanna's story. I also hope it will inspire you to find a way through any difficulties that you may be experiencing. Courage comes from the hand of God, love revolutionizes us, and redemption through Jesus is eternal.

- - -

Printed in Canada